## 'I am not looking for happiness.'

If anyone else had said it Lorne would have felt they were playing a part, perhaps trying to project an image that was mysterious for some diverse purpose of their own. But Francisco *meant* it. The chill increased in strength. He really meant it.

**Dear Reader**

Whatever the weather this summer, come with us to four places in the sun. In this collection, we offer you the romance you love—with the Latin lovers of the Mediterranean...the colourful sights and sounds of Spain...the excitement and glamour of Venice...the natural beauty of Greece...the relaxed, timeless magic of France. A wonderful tour of sensual delight, with four happy endings along the way! Something sultry from Mills & Boon...

*The Editor*

**Helen Brooks** lives in Northamptonshire and is married with three children. As she is a committed Christian, busy housewife and mother, spare time is at a premium but her hobbies include reading, swimming, gardening and walking her two energetic, inquisitive and very endearing young dogs. Her long-cherished aspiration to write became a reality when she put pen to paper on reaching the age of forty, and sent the result off to Mills & Boon.

**Recent titles by the same author:**

AND THE BRIDE WORE BLACK
A HEARTLESS MARRIAGE
BITTER HONEY

# KNIGHT IN BLACK VELVET

BY

## HELEN BROOKS

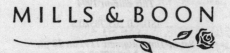

# MILLS & BOON

## MILLS & BOON LIMITED
ETON HOUSE, 18-24 PARADISE ROAD
RICHMOND, SURREY TW9 1SR

*All the characters in this book have no existence outside the imagination of the Author, and have no relation whatsoever to anyone bearing the same name or names. They are not even distantly inspired by any individual known or unknown to the Author, and all the incidents are pure invention.*

*First published in Great Britain 1994 by Mills & Boon Limited*

© Helen Brooks 1994

*Australian copyright 1994   Philippine copyright 1994 This edition 1994*

ISBN 0 263 78520 3

*Set in Times Roman 11½ on 12 pt. 86-9407-48229 C*

*Printed in Great Britain by BPC Paperbacks Ltd A member of The British Printing Company Ltd*

# CHAPTER ONE

'HEY...*señorita*... You lika nice Spanish boy, eh? You wanna say hello maybe?'

Lorne forced her legs, which had increased their pace since the crowd of Spanish youths had started following her into practically a jogging stance, into a slower, calmer rhythm. She mustn't panic! Mustn't give in to this fear that was causing her flesh to prickle with horror. It was broad daylight, for goodness' sake! Admittedly she was in the middle of nowhere on a hot dusty road that seemed to lead into infinity with not a house or building in sight, but they wouldn't *do* anything, would they? The suggestive remarks and cat-calls had grown more daring with the minutes but that didn't mean anything, not really...did it?

'*Señorita*... You *Inglésesa*? *Americana*? You gotta boyfriend, eh?'

The heat was shimmering off the winding road in great waves, the sky an empty vivid blue in which the sun sat like a queen, and Lorne cast yet another desperate glance at the broken chain on her old bike as she marched resolutely forward, pushing her only means of transportation, which was worse than useless, her bulging rucksack rubbing her back and causing the perspiration to trickle between her shoulderblades.

5

'You tired, eh? You wanna rest a little?' They had closed the twenty yard or so gap since she had last turned round; she could feel it in the hairs that were prickling on the back of her neck. What was she going to do? Terror was a huge lump in the base of her throat that restricted breathing and was beginning to make her feel sick. Harsh vivid memories of old headlines flashed into her mind. 'GIRL RAPED AT KNIFE-POINT'. 'FOUR YOUTHS FOUND GUILTY OF THE RAPE OF——' And now it could be her! She could become yet another nameless statistic that would cause most people to click their tongue in sympathy before their eyes ran down the rest of the page. How could she have been so stupid as to put herself in such a vulnerable position?

A burst of ribald laughter just behind her caused her stomach muscles to clench in protest and she wished with all her heart that she had learnt Spanish as the youths continued to shout and encourage each other in their native tongue. But she didn't need to understand what they were saying to know what was on their minds. The thick excited laughter, the shrill note that had entered the young male voices was a portent of things to come.

'Look, why don't you just clear off?' As she swung round she saw her sudden attack had momentarily surprised them as the four young men stopped dead in the road facing her. 'I'm sure you've got better things to do than bother me and frankly you're not funny. OK?'

The narrowing of their eyes and sudden darkening of a couple of the faces told her they understood English far better than she understood Spanish, and also that she had tried the wrong tack. One of the youths, broader and a little older than the rest, stepped forward, his good-looking face surly as he let his dark eyes travel over her body in insolent slowness from the top of her silver-blonde head down to the long, smooth brownness of her legs revealed in their entirety in the old worn denim shorts she was wearing. The only skirt she had brought with her, and which she usually wore every day in spite of the heat to deflect just such a situation as this, had met its end, mangled and torn, in the bicycle chain just a few hours before, necessitating a quick change from the rucksack. 'You think you too good to talk to us, eh?' There was no humour or banter in the youth's voice now. '*Sí*?'

Lorne stared into the hard, unsmiling face as sheer undiluted fear turned her soft grey eyes almost black. The reasons that had driven her to take this long lonely holiday, Sancho's betrayal, along with the resulting humiliation, pain and embarrassment, suddenly seemed to fade into insignificance beside this thing that was about to happen to her. And it was. She knew it.

The same movement that threw the inoffensive bicycle into the middle of the now silent, predatory group watching her so closely also turned her on her feet to run, and it was some seconds before the drum of chasing footsteps sounded on the old dirt road. She ran as she had never run before, as if her life depended on it, which maybe it did, but even as the blood pounded in her ears and she felt the cut of the sharp spiky stones littering the road through her thin black pumps she knew she wasn't going to make it. They were young, fit and strong and they were gaining on her.

The blur of red coming towards her registered a moment before the harsh blaring of the car's horn, but even as she raised her hand in the age-old gesture of appeal for help she twisted her foot on a small boulder and fell, sprawling in the red dirt in a tangle of limbs and long silver-blonde hair and excruciatingly fierce pain. The sandy grit was in her mouth, her eyes, and she could feel the sting of raw flesh on the palms of her hands where she had tried to cushion her fall, but the blinding pain that ripped through her right ankle took every other sensation from her body as she tried to move. For a moment she thought she was going to lose consciousness as the world swirled and flew round her in a dizzying kaleidoscope of colour, but the thought that the approaching car might not have stopped, that she might have been left to the tender mercies of her pursuers, kept her from fainting outright.

By the time she had raised herself into a sitting position at the side of the road she became aware that the car had stopped some yards away, that the four youths were mere racing dots in the distance, and that the occupant of the brilliant red Ferrari was hurrying to her side. The relief made her head swim again and the figure at her side was a blur as he knelt down and took her hands in his. 'Are you injured? Have you hurt yourself?'

She couldn't answer. All her will was concentrated on not making a bigger fool of herself than she had already by being sick at the feet of this Good Samaritan.

'*Habla Inglés*? French? Swedish?'

'I'm English.' The mist was clearing and she took a few long deep breaths before raising her head to focus on the stranger's dark face. 'Thank you for stopping. I was afraid you might not.'

He waved away her thanks with a sharp movement of his hand and as she caught the glimpse of gleaming gold on his wrist from what was obviously a very expensive watch she became aware that he was dressed in formal dinner clothes, the black velvet jacket and dark trousers beautifully cut.

'*Como se llama usted*?'

'I'm sorry, I don't speak Spanish,' she said faintly as the pain in her ankle surged into renewed life when she moved slightly. 'I've been meaning to learn but——'

'Your name?' He was still kneeling at her side and somewhere in the back of her mind she noticed that the austere, coldly handsome face and cool, imperious voice added up to a very disturbing whole.

'Lorne, Lorne Wilson.' For a moment she almost held out her hand in spite of the situation. There was a stark formality, an inherent coldness about the man that was drying up the words in her throat.

'I am Francisco de Vega, Miss Wilson.' Two jet-black eyes pierced her white face. 'Were you alone?'

'Alone?' She stared at him in confusion as she glanced round the empty barren countryside through which the road ran like a winding snake. 'There were these men——'

'I am aware of that.' The voice was sharp and tight. 'I am asking you if there was anyone else with you when this situation developed. A friend, maybe, who was not so fortunate as yourself.'

'Fortunate?' She stared at him as though he were mad. 'Fortunate? I've been followed for miles and hassled and——'

'They did not touch you?' he asked stiffly.

'No.' Her voice was flat now. 'But I was frightened and——'

'Then I repeat, you were fortunate.' The black gaze swept over her again, resting on the tousled blonde hair for a second before meeting her eyes. 'Do you always dress so...indiscreetly when travelling alone?'

'Indiscreetly?' The full import of what he was insinuating caused hot colour to surge into her white face and now her eyes were sparking grey flashes as she raised her head proudly to meet his accusing gaze. 'How I dress is my business, don't you think? Surely I'm entitled——'

'Freedom is a dangerous thing when put in the hands of children,' the dark voice said smoothly, cutting into her furious tirade as though she hadn't spoken. It was the fourth time in as many minutes that he had interrupted her and now all thoughts of gratitude fled as she took in, really took in, for the first time, the proud aristocratic face with its fine aquiline nose, well-shaped thin lips and icy cold eyes. What an overbearing, arrogant, haughty swine of a man! If he thought she needed his help he was very much mistaken!

'Well, thank you for coming to my rescue, Mr de Vega,' Lorne said frostily. 'I'm sorry I seem to have inconvenienced you but I'm fine now so if you'd like to go on your way...' She waved a dismissive hand towards the car in the distance. The effect was spoilt slightly by the fact that she was still sitting in a heap at the side of the road covered in dust and grime and blood from the copious grazes and scratches covering every inch of exposed flesh. And there *was* quite a bit of it. Not that she would ever admit that to him!

'Are all English girls so difficult?' he asked coldly as he rose in one lithe movement to his feet.

'Difficult? I'm not difficult,' she protested sharply, raising her face up and up until she met his eyes. Goodness, she hadn't realised he was so tall, or so broad, or so very... male. Suddenly the Spanish youths seemed like young boys.

'No?' The humourless smile didn't touch the glittering black eyes. 'Has it escaped your notice that your right ankle has swollen to three times its normal size? How, exactly, do you intend to recommence your journey?'

'On my knees if necessary.' Lorne eyed him
tightly. 'I didn't ask to be attacked, you know.
There's no need to be so downright aggressive.'

'Can you stand?' He ignored her defiance with
regal indifference.

'Of course I can.' Her ankle was throbbing so
badly that she could feel it in her head and there
was no way she was going to try to struggle to
her feet in front of his superior gaze. She'd try
when he'd gone. And she hoped it would be soon!
'You are obviously on your way out somewhere.
Thank you again for your assistance and——'

'This is not England, you know.' He eyed her
sourly. 'There won't be a nice safe bus along in
a few minutes to take you where you want to go.
How did you get this far? By taxi?'

'No, I've got...' she paused as her gaze
flickered back down the road '...well...I *did*
have a bike but the chain had broken and then
it probably got more damaged when I threw it at
those louts.'

'You threw your bike at them?' The momentary satisfaction at seeing him lost for words
was sweet. He said something under his breath
in his native tongue that sounded extremely
caustic but the flash of admiration that lit the
black eyes for a brief moment was not lost on
her and it brought her chin up a fraction higher.
She wasn't some pathetic helpless female in spite
of all the evidence to the contrary! And it was
about time he knew it. 'I won't say I understand,
Miss Wilson, because I do not.' He bent down
and lifted her up so swiftly that for a moment

she couldn't believe she was in his arms. 'But one thing I *do* know is that that ankle needs attention and you need a stiff drink after such an unpleasant experience.' In spite of the content of the words his cold stance hadn't mellowed one iota but she was past caring. The pain in her ankle was blazingly fiercely again and she bit her lip until it drew blood in an effort not to cry out.

He glanced once at her white lips as he carried her quickly to the car, placing her in the front seat with a gentleness that belied the grim face. 'What on earth are your parents thinking of to allow such a child to wander about in a strange country like this?'

'Me? Do you mean me?' Now her leg was still again she could just about cope with the pain and her eyes spat fury at his dark face. 'To start with I am not a child, I'm twenty-two and——'

'I do not believe it.' The cool words were not spoken in politeness or as a social comment but stating fact. 'You cannot be a day over seventeen.'

'Look, Mr de Vega...' He slid into the car beside her as she spoke and suddenly the words dried up in her throat. He was so close, so overwhelmingly Latin, so different...

'Francisco.'

'What?' She stared at him, her eyes huge in the paleness of her face from which pain had taken all colour.

'My name is Francisco, Miss Wilson, and let us stop the playing of the game.' It was the first time his excellent English had let him down and she had to stifle the smile that sprang to her lips.

So he was human after all. 'How old are you and how is it that you are all alone in my country?'

'Hang on a minute.' She grabbed at his arm in panic as he started the engine. This could definitely be a case of the frying-pan being much hotter than the fire! 'Where are you taking me?'

Her thoughts were patently visible in both her face and her voice, and the dark, cruel face hardened still further as he glanced down at her. She wished she hadn't touched him. The hard, bunched muscles in his arm spoke of power and authority and just at the moment neither was attractive.

'I am taking you to my home, Miss Wilson, so that your injuries may be attended to and just for the record I am not in the habit of attacking young girls who find themselves at a disadvantage. Do I make myself clear?' His voice was icy and his eyes glittering chips of coal full of righteous contempt as he cast one more withering glance at her frightened face before he carefully removed her hand from his arm and negotiated the car in a semi-circle that brought a cloud of dust wafting into the still hot air.

'You have not answered my question.' They were travelling at a breakneck speed along the empty road and the suddenness of the change in her circumstances coupled with the sickening pain in her ankle was causing Lorne to feel more than a little light-headed.

'I'm sorry?' She cast a questioning glance at the harsh profile.

'I doubt it. I doubt if that emotion has ever been a particular weakness of yours. Don't you realise how stupid——?' He stopped abruptly. 'How old are you, really, and how is it that you are travelling alone?'

'I told you.' She cast an exasperated glance at the dark profile but as she let her eyes rest on the handsome, cold face something jerked deep inside her and she snapped her eyes away quickly. 'I am twenty-two, whether you believe it or not. I've got my passport in my rucksack; I'll prove it.'

'That is not necessary.' He raised a bronzed hand for a second from the leather-clad steering-wheel. 'I am going to take you to my house in order for your ankle to receive attention and then I will arrange for you to be driven to your place of accommodation. *Si?*'

'Look, please don't bother, Mr de Vega.' Lorne was feeling more uncomfortable by the second. Where on earth was his house anyway and how could she tell him she had run out of money a couple of days ago and was making the small amount she had left make do for the next few days by sleeping under the stars? 'If you could just drop me somewhere where I can get my bike mended . . . My bike!' Her voice was so shrill that he jumped visibly. 'We must go back; I've left my bike——'

'An old bicycle, and damaged, you said?' The car didn't slow down. 'It has let you down this time, which could have resulted in a tragedy. I suggest you get yourself a new bicycle, Miss

Wilson, or travel about on your excursions in a
taxi like everyone else. *Sí*?'

'No!' she all but shouted at him and the hard
square jaw stiffened into concrete. 'You must go
back; I can't get another bike; please...'

'I have no intention of returning from whence
I have come,' he said tightly. 'I am already very
late for an important business appointment and
do not wish to miss my dinner engagement in
addition.'

'But you don't understand...' Her voice trailed
away as he raised one black sardonic eyebrow in
caustic agreement.

'On that point you are right, Miss Wilson,' he
said silkily, 'but whether I understand or not for
once in your life you are going to do as you are
told. You have already proved you aren't safe to
be let out alone. You can telephone your hotel
and speak to whoever is waiting there for you
and explain the situation. And then my chauffeur
will drive you to wherever you want to go.'

'Your chauffeur?' she asked weakly. He didn't
reply and she sank back into the soft leather seat
helplessly. If she told him she had no hotel, no
transport, no money and only the clothes she
stood up in with a change of underclothes and a
clean T-shirt in the rucksack it would confirm
every low opinion he had of her. She would have
to brazen it out somehow, she had no choice, but
where was she going to sleep tonight and how
soon could she get back to rescue the remains of
her bike?

She had been so immersed in her thoughts that she had barely taken note of her surroundings, but now she saw that the unfenced rocky land stretching away on both sides of the dusty road was growing greener. Where exactly were they? She wrinkled her brow. She had left the town of Extremadura several days ago after pottering around there for a week soaking up the history of the place. She had heard that the harsh environment of south-west Spain had been the cradle of the conquistadors, the home of the men who had opened up new worlds for the Spanish empire in the golden age when the heroes had returned with their spoils of gold and fabulous wealth to live in ornate splendour and fabulous luxury, and it hadn't disappointed her. But after several weeks of exploring historically rich towns and feeding her mind and eyes on imperial palaces, crumbling fortresses and churches and impressive monuments she had felt the need to recharge her batteries in peace and quiet. An English tourist had mentioned the Coto Doñana National Park and she had decided to travel in that direction. An unwise decision, with hindsight!

As the car slowed and turned into a narrow man-made road leading through a sweet-smelling pine forest she darted another glance at the man sitting next to her so silently. 'We are nearly there,' he said quietly. 'I have medication that will ease the worst of the pain.'

'It's all right,' she said quickly. 'I'm fine really.' He didn't even bother to reply to such an inane remark and she couldn't really blame him. She glanced down at her swollen ankle in frustration. What if it was broken? What would she do? She would have to find a British consul somehow, contact Tom in England...oh, hell, what a mess! And things had just begun to work out. She had just been able to sleep again the last few nights without thoughts of Sancho and Janie taunting her like tiny needles...

As they passed through massive open gates set in a high stone wall the feeling of apprehension intensified. The car scrunched along a pristinely clean drive between immaculate opulent gardens festooned with flowers and shrubs and bordered in the distance with orange, lemon and fig trees. As she saw the palatial mansion in the distance the heat in her cheeks spread all over her body. This wasn't his home, was it? It was like every stately home she had seen in England rolled into one, and even then some.

'Is this...?' She paused and licked dry lips. 'Is this your home?'

'*Sí.*' They were approaching the house now and the evening sunshine, still hot and fierce, sent countless shadows over the mellowed stone from the massive oak and cedar trees shading the high walls. The house was huge, stretching endlessly in Moorish beauty rich with turrets, decorative iron fretwork and tiny, exquisitely wrought towers that had been used to maximum aesthetic affect. The geometrical design formed by the mock-battlements and different shades of stone was offset by the blaze of colour from the climbing

vines that had found their way over most of the
house's exterior forming vivid splashes of
crimson, mauve and pink against dark green fo-
liage. It was beautiful, it was unreal and it fitted
this man perfectly.

'Sit still, Miss Wilson.' His voice was terse and
he had uncoiled himself from the car and appeared at her side almost in one movement, lifting
her from the interior in spite of her protestations
that she could walk. 'Please do not be ridiculous.' He glanced down at her as he carried
her up the deep stone steps that led up to a
beautifully carved front door that was a work of
art in itself, complete with an impressive coat of
arms, and she saw his eyes weren't really black
but of such a deep dark brown that they appeared so. She had always thought brown eyes
were soft and appealing in the past but these eyes
were of a different hue. Hard, brilliantly alert,
they had all the softness of glittering steel.

The door opened as they reached the top step
and two uniformed maids appeared in the en-
trance, fluttering agitatedly before being called
abruptly into order by a rapier-sharp voice behind
them. 'Señor de Vega.' A tall, stately looking man
pushed the women aside as he hurried to take
Lorne from Francisco's arms but Francisco
merely barked a few words in rapid Spanish as
he walked with her into a room leading off the
huge marble hall. She had never seen so much
marble in her life—the floors, the walls, the
magnificent winding staircase, all in dusky-pink-
veined marble. But she had no time to reflect on

what she was seeing. As Francisco deposited her
gently on a long low couch the manservant was
back again carrying a small black bag.

'*Gracias, Alfonso.*'

'That looks like a doctor's bag.' She tried to
smile but the whole situation had robbed her of
her normal intrinsic vivacity; in fact she had never
felt so frightened or overwhelmed in all her life.
Something of what she was feeling must have
communicated itself to the tall man in front of
her because Francisco's voice was more mellow
as he spoke.

'It is a doctor's bag. I qualified ten years ago.'

'You're a doctor?' She raised startled grey eyes
to meet the piercing blackness of his.

'I said I qualified, that is all. Events happened
which determined I was not able to follow my
chosen profession. However, I think I still remember enough for this circumstance.' He gave
a small smile, but it was a real smile this time,
and for a second his face was illuminated as
though someone had turned on a light, and then
he was kneeling at her feet as he lifted her foot
into his hand, the black velvet dinner-jacket
making the situation seem even more unreal. A
doctor who wasn't a doctor living in a house that
was beyond most people's wildest dreams—— She
gasped as a shaft of pain cut into her thoughts.

'It is painful, yes?' Francisco raised his face as
he spoke and then she was looking down on him
again, his bent head with its shock of tight curly
black hair giving her the strangest feeling in the
pit of her stomach. And there was the feel of his

warm flesh as he gently moulded and kneaded her foot. It was...unsettling. 'I do not think you have any broken bones.' He rose as he spoke after gently placing her foot back on the couch. 'But what you do have is probably more painful than a break. I think the ligaments and tendons have been badly torn and the swelling is very severe. I would suggest you ask your hotel receptionist to make arrangements for X-rays to be taken at the local hospital to be on the safe side, of course, but possibly two or three weeks of rest will return the foot to new. Now, you wish to telephone your hotel?'

'No, no, thank you, it's all right.' She had spoken too quickly and saw the small frown of puzzlement between his eyes with a feeling of alarm. 'If someone could just take me back I'll be fine...really. You must leave now; you're already late and——'

'A drink?' He cut into her stumbling speech abruptly as his eyes flashed over her face. For a spine-chilling moment she had the feeling he could read her mind and then shrugged the ridiculous notion away. She was imagining things and she was normally so level-headed. What was the matter with her? 'Brandy is good for the nerves, or maybe you would prefer a glass of wine or a soft drink?' Francisco continued quietly. 'And I will give you something for the pain.'

'Please, you just go, I've delayed you enough already...' Her voice stumbled to a halt as he searched her features with another long, considering glance before turning to pull the long bell-cord at one side of the magnificent ornate fireplace.

When Alfonso entered seconds later Francisco spoke to him in rapid Spanish before extracting a bottle from the black bag and handing Lorne two small white tablets. 'Alfonso is bringing you a glass of iced water.'

'Thank you.' She looked up at him with a small smile but the hard face eyed her coldly without a glimmer of warmth.

'And then I suggest you and I have a chat, Miss Wilson.'

'Lorne.' She didn't try a smile this time; she had the feeling nothing would penetrate that icy mind. 'The name is Lorne.'

'As you wish.' He inclined his head before walking over to the huge cocktail cabinet on the far side of the room and pouring what looked like brandy into a cut-crystal goblet. 'Will you join me?'

'No, thank you.' Alfonso returned at that moment with the water and she thanked him with a warm smile before turning back to Francisco. 'This will be fine.' As she swallowed the tiny tablets under the hard black gaze her eyes wandered round the luxurious room, which was furnished exquisitely in varying shades of silver and grey with small occasional tables in dark polished wood to offset the pale carpet. People actually lived like this, she thought disbelievingly. The wealth contained in this room alone would keep her for the rest of her life!

'Now, Lorne.' The sound of her name on his lips brought her head snapping round to meet his gaze. 'I am going to ask you some questions and I want truthful answers. Is that understood?' His voice was cool and tight.

She stared at him without answering. She had always disliked authoritative people, whether male or female, but he took the word to another dimension! Just who did he think he was anyway? He might be king-pin in this little corner of the world but if he thought he could bully her he was very much mistaken! Her chin lifted slightly with her thoughts.

'Your name is Lorne Wilson and you are twenty-two years of age?' She nodded slowly. 'Where are you staying and who are you travelling with?'

'Look, Mr de Vega, I'm very grateful for your assistance this evening but could we just leave it at that?' she asked quietly, keeping all irritation out of her voice. 'I'm a grown woman and quite capable of taking care of myself. In fact——'

'It looked like it.' Now his voice was biting. 'Do you not realise what a narrow escape you had, girl? You are such a tiny little thing, you would not have stood a chance against those men if things had got difficult.'

'Well, it didn't come to that, did it?' she said flatly. 'And I repeat, I am very grateful to you for appearing at the right time but I would like to go back now, please.'

'Back where?' His eyes had narrowed and she suddenly felt he knew...he knew she had nowhere to stay. 'Exactly where, Lorne?' She stared at him dumbly as her mind raced, trying to come up with a plausible answer. 'I am not an idiot so please stop attempting to treat me like one.' He downed his drink in one swallow and walked over to the cabinet, pouring another good measure into his glass before turning to face her again. 'You are one of these student people, is that it?' The beautifully modulated voice was scathing. 'Thumbing a lift here and there, living reck-lessly——'

'I have *not* been thumbing lifts,' she said in-dignantly. 'I told you, I had my bike.'

'Ah, yes, the bicycle.' He walked over and knelt down beside her so that his dark face was a breath away. 'But you have the bicycle no longer, do you, so how do you intend to manage, especially with that ankle? You have nowhere to stay tonight, do you? Answer me.'

'No.' The word had been forced out against her volition; there was something in those black eyes that was mesmerising. He relaxed then, sinking back on his heels as he eyed her coldly, shaking his head a little as he rose.

'And you are by yourself.' It was a statement and she didn't bother to confirm what he knew. 'I cannot believe this.' He stood looking down at her as she lay on the couch, his long, muscled legs slightly apart and his hands on his hips. 'Don't you realise how vulnerable you are? You look about sixteen, all hair and eyes, and you seem intent on displaying as much of that...

attractive body as you can. I really do not believe——'

'It's not my fault my skirt got caught in the bike chain,' she said weakly. When he had knelt down so close the smell of him had been intoxicating and her senses were still coping with the shock of it. She didn't like him, in fact he was one of the coldest, rudest people she had ever met in her entire life, but whatever he was he was all male.

'Your skirt?' He waved his hand irritably. 'What has your skirt got to do with anything?'

'Everything!' Suddenly it was all too much. Sancho's desertion, Janie's betrayal, the shock and terror of the preceding hours and the pain in her ankle culminated in a break in the dam that she had been holding in for weeks. She didn't recognise the wailing noise was coming from her at first but as the tears coursed down her face and her last scrap of control went with them she knew she was making a terrible fool of herself, but suddenly she didn't care. She didn't care about anything any more. She was tired of being brave, tired of coping on her own, tired of trying to keep going, just altogether, totally, absolutely tired.

## CHAPTER TWO

'HERE.' The big white hankerchief was thrust under Lorne's nose at the same time as she became aware that Francisco had sat down beside her, pulling her head on to the broad expanse of his chest as his other hand stroked her hair comfortingly. 'Whatever it is it cannot be as bad as all that, little one.' The unexpected kindness made her worse and it was some considerable time later before she had composed herself enough to raise a tear-drenched face from its soft resting place.

'I've ruined your jacket.' She looked aghast at the wet velvet streaked with dirt from her fall on the road, but Francisco smiled slowly, his dark face enigmatic.

'It is of no consequence.' He moved his arm from her shoulders as he shrugged off the jacket, slinging it casually on the floor. The snowy white shirt it revealed accentuated broad shoulders and a hard-muscled chest, and as he rose and fetched her a glass of neat brandy she felt something leap in her body that made her flesh tingle. 'Drink that, all of it, and then I think we must have the—how do you say it—chat, *sí*?' He didn't sit beside her again, standing just in front of her after handing her the drink, his dark face expressionless.

'You must think I'm mad...' She took a long gulp of the brandy and then choked helplessly. 'I'm sorry, I'm not used to this.'

'That is one thing in your favour,' he said drily. 'And now, Miss Lorne Wilson, you will begin at the beginning. How is it that you are all alone with no money?' He raised questioning eyebrows. 'I presume you have no money?'

'Not much,' she admitted slowly. 'That's why I hadn't stayed anywhere. I thought I could just manage if I slept out in the open somewhere and eked out the food.'

'You thought you could just manage?' He shook his head slowly. 'And how long have you been "just managing"?'

'A while.' She sniffed dismally. 'I was just going to have a look at the Coto Doñana National Park and then think about going home.'

'Have a look...?' His voice trailed away in a mixture of disgust and wonder. 'Do you realise how vast that place is? It is not somewhere that one wanders alone. Maybe a guided tour or something similar but the lynx and wild boar that lodge there would be very pleased to make your acquaintance on a dark night. It is a wild place, Lorne, not suitable for a little English girl with hair like spun silver and wrists that one could snap in a second.' As he gazed at her something dark and warm in his face caught and held her eyes and the moment stretched until he shook his head suddenly, a shadow passing over his face that turned it cold and withdrawn. 'This is crazy.' The muttered words held a note of anger and the hostility was back in his voice when he spoke next. 'Start at the beginning.'

'I came to Spain eight weeks ago with some friends,' she began slowly, the chill that had entered his voice making her suddenly lonelier than she had felt for days. 'There were four of us who have just graduated from university and we thought it would be fun to travel a bit, take some time out for a year or so.'

'That would be fun, yes,' he agreed with shuttered eyes.

'But it didn't work out.' She was beginning to flounder and he would think she was trying to hide something, but how could she possibly explain to this cold, austere man how happy she had been when Sancho had suggested showing her his homeland? She had only got to know him in the last few weeks of university life although she had admired him from afar for the last four years, but he had always had a different model-girl type on his arm every time she had seen him. And then it had been *her* on his arm and she had been wild with delight and all her friends had been green with envy. Especially Janie. Janie... with her long red hair, even longer nails and come-to-bed eyes. But she had seemed so happy with Steve and they had been going out together for nearly a year. Even now it was hard to believe——

'It didn't work out?' The deep voice with its foreign accent brought her back to the present with a jolt and she shook her blonde head slowly.

'No.' That was the understatement of the year, she thought grimly. When Sancho had endorsed Janie's suggestion that she and Steve join them on the tour round Spain she had been delighted. The financial saving had been considerable and it had all worked out fine, or so she had thought. How naïve could a person be? That was what Janie had thrown at her when Lorne had found her best friend and Sancho in bed together. Steve had left on the next flight home but she had been determined to complete the proposed trip. No one was going to send her skulking home like a whipped dog with its tail between its legs, least of all an over-sexed Spaniard and a tramp of an English girl.

'Would you care to elaborate on that?'

She shook her head again as she looked him straight in the eyes. 'I can't, I really can't. Suffice it to say one of us went home, the other two are in the south of Spain somewhere and I'm here. We were touring, on our bikes,' she finished weakly.

'Well, as an explanation it is pretty poor but I suppose it will do,' he said sardonically. 'The final line is that you are now injured, homeless and without funds?'

'That's about it.' She eyed him warily.

'There is an English word that describes you very well,' he said coolly, 'and I really cannot think of a suitable substitute in Spanish. The word is dimwit. Have you heard it?'

'How dare you?' She winced visibly as the sudden jerk of anger tweaked her ankle. 'Look,

you said you would run me back to my hotel; it's
no different if you get me back to my bike and
I can take it from there.'

'The hell it is.' His accent made the words
almost attractive. 'I do not know what sort of
men you are used to running around with, Lorne
Wilson, and frankly I think I would prefer not
to know——' his eyes flashed condemningly over
her bare legs in the brief shorts '—but you are
now my responsibility and I do not intend to send
you off into the night like a bird with a broken
wing. You are clearly quite incapable of looking
after yourself; in fact I think a child of ten would
have more sense than you. You will stay here
tonight and we will review the situation in the
morning.'

'What?' She stared at him with big saucer eyes,
ignoring the insults for the moment.

'And I think we can probably provide something more... suitable for you to wear in the
meantime.' His nose all but wrinkled. 'My sister
has her own apartment here when she pays a visit
and although considerably taller she is as slender
as you.'

'There's no need for that and——'

'Oh, but there is,' he corrected tightly. 'This
is not a tourist resort and you may have noticed
that young females do not display themselves
quite so wantonly in this part of Spain. The
young men who followed you probably thought,
quite legitimately, that you were encouraging
them to do so, especially in view of the fact that
you were not accompanied.'

'Well, that's just plain ridiculous,' she said angrily as her temper rose to boiling-point. 'Do you mean to tell me that women here have to be covered from head to foot? What are you living in, for crying out loud, the Dark Ages? Women should be able to dress exactly how they want to without becoming targets for the sort of animals that followed me.'

'Not a feminist too?' He shut his eyes briefly and she was furious with herself for noticing, at such a time as this, that his eyelashes were incredibly long and curly as they rested for a moment on the hard, tanned cheeks. 'I really think I need another brandy and then I must make a telephone call. But first you need to refresh yourself. Teresa and Benita will help you bathe and then I will put a bandage on that ankle to try and contain the swelling.'

'But you have to go out,' she said faintly. 'You said——'

'I think I realised when I picked you up off the road that my evening was not going to plan,' he said drily. 'Now please allow me, if not as a man then as a doctor, to take care of you tonight. Tomorrow we can arrange the hospital visit and organise accommodation and a ticket home.'

'But why are you helping me like this?' She stared at him, her grey eyes huge and liquid in her tear-smudged face and her silky blonde hair a cascade of silver falling over slender shoulders. 'You don't have to...'

'In my country we do not forget the rules of hospitality,' he said coldly after a long pregnant

moment when he had searched her face with his
piercing eyes. 'You are a stranger in my land and
you are in need, it is as simple as that. Also the
fact that I cannot understand how you have not
been eaten alive before now compels me not to—
how would you put it?—push your luck?'

'Eaten alive?' There was a darkness in his face
that frightened her. 'But there are no wild animals in this part of Spain, are there?'

'The human animal is far more ferocious than
any wild cat when its appetite is aroused,' he said
grimly, 'and unfortunately often less noble.'

'Oh . . .' As burning colour flooded her cheeks
at the memory of the Spanish youths' hot eyes
and predatory mouths she dropped her eyes
quickly. He thought her a fool, a complete and
utter fool, and she was beginning to agree with
him.

An hour later, bathed, creamed and with her
hair newly washed, she lay on the vast bed in the
suite of rooms she had been shown to with her
head spinning and her mind racing. After the two
maids had helped her to bath and wash her hair
they had half carried her to the bed where she
had found a pair of trousers, a thigh-length
blouse in raw silk and even a change of underwear
laid out for her. The wildly expensive clothes so
casually given, the unimaginable wealth all
around her that spoke of power and authority on
a scale she had never touched before and the cold,
fierce personality of the man who seemed to be
master of this empire was numbing her mind.
What have you blundered into? she asked herself

soberly as she glanced again round the fabulous room. The sooner she was out of here the better. She had never been a snob in even the mildest sense of the word but she had to admit that this particular situation had, temporarily, overwhelmed her.

A light knock on the closed door brought her out of her reverie and, thinking it was one of the maids again, she called for them to enter. As the door opened and Francisco's tall, broad shape stood framed in the doorway, her heart jumped painfully in her chest. He had changed since she last saw him and the black silk shirt and casual black jeans that he now wore seemed to project still further the innate cold austerity of the man while adding to the cruel, handsome face a piratical effect. For a moment she could have believed they had travelled back in time and she was facing one of the original conquistadors, fiercely proud, intrinsically cruel and without mercy.

'Don't look so frightened.' It was the last thing she expected him to say and as her mouth opened in a small O of surprise she saw a fleeting smile touch the firm, hard mouth. 'If all my patients would have reacted like you I think it is probably as well fate led me in another direction than that of a doctor, do you not agree?'

'I'm sorry.' She pulled herself together with a visible effort as he walked slowly across the room, carrying his bag.

'Is it still as painful?' After examining the swollen flesh that was already turning a faint blue he began to wind a tight bandage expertly round her foot.

'No, no, it's not,' she said quickly, trying to concentrate on the ache in her ankle rather than the feel of his warm, competent fingers on her skin. The sight of this severe, forbidding man performing such a gentle task was such an antithesis that it was causing her heart to pound again. She didn't know why he affected her so strongly but affect her he did, and she found it acutely disturbing.

'The clothes are lovely,' she said after a few seconds, more for something to say than anything else. The silence had begun to scream at her.

'Good.' He raised his head as he spoke after tying the bandage lightly in place. 'I thought they would fit with a little adjustment.' His eyes glanced at the trousers that she had rolled up a few inches.

In spite of herself she couldn't stop a pink flush from staining her cheeks at the thought of the tiny scraps of lacy underwear spread out on the bed. The female shape was clearly no mystery to him. Again, it was as though he could read her mind.

'There is no need to be embarrassed.' The cool voice was mocking but not unfriendly. 'I have not reached the age of thirty-eight without having become ... familiar with the items ladies wear under their clothing.'

'I don't doubt it,' she said as lightly as the hectic flush in her cheeks would allow, 'but I'm not used to men choosing my clothes for me.'

He stiffened as he looked down at her, her long silver hair spread out in a shining pillow round her head and her slender shape defenceless in the middle of the huge bed.

'I do not play with children, Miss Lorne Wilson, so you may let your anxiety lessen.' His voice was expressionless and she couldn't read anything beyond the black glitter in his eyes. 'You have had one distressing experience today; let that suffice.'

'What does that mean?' she asked hotly. 'That you consider me a child? You still don't believe I am twenty-two, is that it?'

'Your numerical age has nothing to do with it,' he said calmly, 'or even the fact that you look about five years younger than you are. I can read in your eyes, your body, your whole outlook on life that the world hasn't touched you with its unpleasant, darker side yet. That is good; you must hold on to that for as long as you can and be with companions of like mind.'

'And you aren't?' She didn't know what made her ask such a pertinent question but it was out before she could hold it back. He froze for an infinitesimal moment and then breathed out slowly, his eyes hooded.

'I'm not,' he agreed grimly, his eyes softening a little as they took in her bewildered young face. 'Stay in the sunshine for as long as you can, my little English *infanta*, the shadows will beckon soon enough.'

'*Infanta*?' She didn't like this constant reference to the fact that he considered her incapable of behaving in an adult fashion. Admittedly she might have made a mistake in trying to travel round a foreign country by herself without knowing the language but she had survived rather well, all things considered! She was past the age of consent, she was no child, and she was sick of his superior, condemning attitude! 'What does *infanta* mean?' she asked testily. 'Infant, baby, I suppose?'

'Not at all.' He had settled back against the pillar of the four-poster bed, his arms crossed and his face devoid of all expression. 'It means princess. You see, I was not being insulting.'

'Well, that makes a change.' She found she suddenly couldn't control her tongue at all. The need to prove that she wasn't completely stupid, that she could manage her own affairs very well, was goading her on. 'I'm not quite the little innocent you seem to be making me out to be, you know,' she said crossly. 'I've had four years at a university doing an English degree for which I got a 2-1; that's pretty good incidentally.' He raised dark eyebrows but said nothing. 'And I supported myself the whole time, working in the holidays to supplement my grant. *I* arranged my lodgings when necessary, *I* dealt with any financial problems, *I* have taken care of my life for the last few years.'

'Why?' The one word stopped her flow and she stared at him. 'Why has it been necessary for you to do all that? Where are your parents, your family?'

'My parents died when I was ten,' she said flatly, 'and I lived with my older brother and his wife and family till I left for university at eighteen. They haven't much money, they couldn't afford to support me; besides, Tom has health problems and they've got enough difficulties of their own without worrying about me.'

'There is no other family?' he asked quietly, his eyes watching her every expression.

'Not really.' She shrugged slender shoulders. 'Besides, I like looking after myself. In spite of what you may be thinking, I usually do it quite well, too.'

'Do you indeed?' She had no idea of the ethereal, delicate picture she made lying on the large bed, her hair a shining mass of silver and her small, heart-shaped face pale against the dark orange of the silk shirt. Finely boned and small, she had always disliked her slimness and lack of height, but to the dark, bronzed man watching her so intently she was breathtakingly lovely. 'And men?' His voice was still cool but with a husky note now that made her stomach tremble. 'Where have men fitted into this independent life?'

'I've had boyfriends,' she said defiantly as she raised herself to a sitting position against the mass of soft, deep blue pillows. 'Quite a few, as it happens; in fact it was my last boyfriend who brought me to Spain in the first place.'

'I see.' He moved to her side again and bent to pick up the bag lying on the floor. 'Then maybe I was mistaken in my opinion about you. Maybe you are a woman of the world, used to dealing with life and love in the modern fashion? Uncaring, hard; are you like that, little *infanta*?'

As he raised his head on a level with hers their eyes locked and as he slowly bent towards her with a smothered groan it was as though he was fighting something deep within himself, the turmoil he was feeling reflected in the darkness of his face.

Her heart began to pound and the blood raced madly through her veins in an agony of excitement. She had wanted this to happen from the first moment she had seen him, she realised with a little shock of horror, had wanted to know what the feel of his lips would be like.

He rested his hands either side of her slim shape as he took her mouth in a gentle, exploratory kiss that changed within seconds as he felt her mouth quiver beneath his. His lips became hard, demanding, and she felt her bones turn to water at the deeply searching invasion of his mouth. No other man had kissed her like this before! The thought burnt into her mind at the same moment as she shuddered against him, unable to resist the powerful desire that was sending shafts of pleasure trembling through her body.

As he felt her response he lowered himself on to the bed until he was lying above her, close

enough for her to feel his evident arousal but
without the full weight of his body resting against
hers. She couldn't believe that another human
being was making her feel like this as frantic, hot
excitement had her tumbling into another dimension. Before Sancho most of her dates had
been nonentities with a relatively chaste embrace
on the doorstep; in fact she knew she had gained
something of a reputation for being an icy cool
blonde. Sancho had made her feel different but
even he hadn't got past that certain something
that had made her call a halt to his lovemaking
before it got out of hand. She had known that
one of the reasons he had suggested the Spanish
trip was to overcome her resistance. But it hadn't
been necessary. Janie had had no such
inhibitions.

The thought didn't have the power to touch
her at all; all her emotions, all her senses, were
tied up in a whirlwind of touch and smell. She
wasn't aware of the bewildered note in her cry as
his hands on her skin made her moan against the
hard face but suddenly, abruptly, he had lifted
himself from her and was standing away before
walking across to the other side of the room.

'Do you see now?' His voice was deep and violent. 'I was right, was I not? You have not yet
made the transition into full awareness—you are
a child after all.' The hard reality of his words
hit her painfully as she stared into the glittering
black eyes. He seemed angry, furiously angry,
and she didn't understand why. She hadn't
pushed him away, hadn't told him to stop...'

'I do not need a complication like you in my life,' he said tightly. 'I should never have brought you here. I should have left you back there, on the road.'

'But I don't understand,' she whispered dazedly. 'What have I done wrong?' How could he be so hostile, so cold, when just a few minutes before...?

'You think you would enjoy a nice little flirtation in this safe little world in which you live?' he asked grimly. 'Is that what you think? But I am not one of your college friends with the time to court and woo you and persuade you into my bed. And there are others like me out there. Go home, Miss Lorne Wilson. Go back to where it is safe and controlled and ordinary before you find yourself hurt badly. You are a lamb among wolves here.'

The slam of the door reverberated round the room and she was still staring at it minutes later as she tried to take in what had happened. His words had lashed her but even as she thought about them she didn't fully understand why he had been so enraged.

She hadn't been the one to pull away, she hadn't initiated the embraces in the first place, and it had been Francisco who had insisted she accompany him home despite her protests. She relaxed against the pillows after a long, taut moment, shutting her eyes as her head hammered with images and harsh, cruel words.

'This is all unreal,' she muttered dazedly as she settled deeper into the soft bed. He was unreal;

this magnificent, larger than life house was unreal; she would wake up soon from this crazy dream and find herself curled up under a tree somewhere as she had done the last few days on the road. That was it, it *was* a dream, a strange and worrying and curiously thrilling dream ... It was her last coherent thought before sleep overtook her.

this is difficult, larger than life things was
wrote; she would wake up soon from this crazy
dream and find herself curled up under a tree
somewhere as she had done the last few days on
the road. That must be it: a dream, a strange
and worrying and curiously thrilling dream.

## CHAPTER THREE

THE tap on the door brought Lorne instantly
awake and fully alert in a moment as though part
of her mind had been keeping watch all the time.
The room was dark, full of a rich, heavy dusk
that carried the perfume of sweet-scented jasmine
and verbena from the open window. Another
gentle knock compelled her to answer and as
Alfonso's grey head appeared round the door she
breathed a sigh of relief. She needed to compose
herself and get her thoughts in order before she
faced Francisco again.

'Señor de Vega wishes me to inform you that
dinner will be served in the main dining-room in
half an hour,' the elderly manservant said with
formal politeness. 'Benita or Teresa will come to
take you downstairs and the *señor* thought these
may be useful to you.' He produced a pair of
crutches like a magician from behind his back.
It was clear from both his attitude and his unsmiling face that he heartily disapproved of this
waif that his master had brought home, and as
Lorne smiled her thanks the stiff façade didn't
crack by so much as a glimmer. 'Half an hour,
then, *señorita*.' As the door shut, Lorne sank
back on the bed again for a second before
switching on the bedside lamp. At once the room
was filled with a soft warm light and as she

hobbled to the chair where Alfonso had propped the crutches her ankle reminded her that for the moment, at least, she was dependent on the harsh, cold master of this place for her every need.

Should she telephone Tom? Even as the thought materialised she dismissed it. She had spent the last four years managing on her own and trying to convince him that she was no longer his responsibility. The shock of her parents' death in a car accident, the arrival of another mouth to feed in addition to his four children and then severe business worries had culminated in her brother's first heart attack at the young age of thirty-nine just a year before she left for college. His financial burdens were still considerable and although a happy family life alleviated some of the strain she still worried constantly about the state of his health. No—she shook her head determinedly—she wouldn't contact Tom. She would manage this herself; she had no choice.

'You are managing the crutches very well.' As she limped into the huge ornate dining-room with Teresa at her elbow Francisco rose immediately from an easy-chair at the far end of the room and moved quickly to her side, his dark face carefully expressionless. 'Come and sit down; dinner will be served shortly. Would you care for a glass of wine, sherry?'

'Sherry would be lovely, thank you.' She sank gratefully into a wide cushioned chair and flexed her arms for a moment. She had concentrated so fiercely on her balance in order not to go sprawling at his feet that she hadn't looked at his face, but now as he handed her the beautiful crystal wine glass her eyes met his and the sensation that passed through her body was like a small electric shock.

In the bright light from the magnificent glittering chandelier overhead that dominated the embossed carved ceiling he looked even more dangerous than she remembered. There was a darkness about him, an almost primitive power that seemed to be waiting to break forth from the surface veneer of civilisation. A small shiver snaked down her spine. He was handsome, yes, and that tall, lean body would cause any woman to turn for a second glance, but the aura of cold authority and remoteness that sat on him like a second skin was undeniably chilling. This man would be capable of almost anything. Once the thought had formed she knew it was true. Almost anything...

'I have delayed dinner for a few minutes in order to talk to you in private.' As he pulled a chair close to hers and leant forward she stared at him in naked apprehension before forcing a quick smile to her lips.

'Oh, dear, what have I done now?'

He didn't respond to her smile but his eyes were like warm velvet as they moved slowly over her pale skin, resting for a minute on the silvery sheen of her hair before returning to meet hers. 'You have done nothing, Lorne. The fault is mine.'

However could she have thought his eyes were hard? she thought dazedly. Suddenly his whole face was warmer, tender, and for a moment she could see why he would have been a perfect doctor. The transformation was bewildering. Just when she had thought she had got him all taped he had metamorphosed in front of her very eyes.

'I have never behaved in such a reprehensible manner towards a guest in my home before—do you believe that?' She couldn't reply, her mind didn't seem to be functioning, but her small nod seemed to satisfy him. 'I would like to offer you my apologies and to assure you that it will not happen again. It was the very opposite of what I intended——' He broke off abruptly. 'Quite inexcusable.'

She swallowed hard and then smiled more naturally although his last words had caused a small pang of she knew not what. 'I'm sorry too; I seem to have caused a great deal of trouble. You've missed your appointments...' Her voice trailed away. 'I'm not usually so stupid.'

'I am sure you are not but we are not discussing your actions,' he said softly as he took one of her hands in his, looking down at its tininess in his large hands before setting it back abruptly in her lap. 'Do you forgive me, Lorne, for behaving little better than your pursuers?'

'Yes, it's all right, you didn't...' Why did she blush so easily? she thought wretchedly. She must resemble a boiled lobster at the moment whereas he was devastatingly cool and controlled, his dark eyes searching her face with something in their depths she couldn't read.

Dinner was served ten minutes later and when she was seated at the shiny dark wood dining-table in which the place settings of silver and exquisite arrangements of flowers that festooned the table were reflected in perfect detail the unreal feeling came back, stronger than before. This time yesterday she had been curled up under a somewhat prickly bush on soft sand looking up into a sky that was a dark blanket alive with a pulsing tapestry of stars, and trying to convince herself that the rustlings and movements in the undergrowth near by were her imagination and that the rumbling hunger pains in her stomach were good for her soul.

There were certainly no hunger pains tonight, she thought wryly as she finished the first course of gazpacho, a refreshing cold soup, made from tomato, cucumber, olive oil, bread, garlic and other seasonings and chilled with ice. It was delicious, the best she had tasted since coming to Spain, but she felt so tense and awkward seated opposite Francisco at the vast dining-table being waited on by the attentive Benita and Teresa that she had a job to force the food down.

Francisco sat in enigmatic silence, lounging comfortably in his seat, his dark eyes lazy as they wandered over her face now and again and his big body relaxed. Looking at him now she couldn't believe the scene in the bedroom when the cold mask had been ripped aside and blazing passion had taken its place but neither was he the cold, austere stranger who had rescued her on the road. Who was he? What was he? He seemed to have a mask for every eventuality and she had the feeling she hadn't even begun to see the real Francisco de Vega.

'Have you lived here long?' They had started on the second course of fresh lobster with aubergine salad and *patatas bravas*—spicy potatoes—and she felt she just had to break the silence that was grinding at her overwrought nerves.

'The estate has been in my family for generations,' Francisco said quietly. 'I inherited it on my father's death ten years ago.'

'Oh.' She smiled uncertainly. 'Well, it's very beautiful, very Moorish somehow.'

He nodded, his black eyes closed and hooded against her as their glittering light moved over her face again. 'The Arabs ruled my country for hundreds of years and the Phoenicians, Greeks and Romans all claimed it for their own. Even now the separate kingdoms which made up the original Spanish nation remain very much in evidence in a diversity of language, culture and artistic traditions. You may have appreciated that in your travels?' She nodded slowly as his deep rich voice continued. 'Our history encompasses the Romans, Moors and the "Golden Age" of Renaissance imperialism and in certain parts villages have changed little since Columbus set sail. Most true Spaniards can trace their origins for centuries.'

'And are you a true Spaniard?' she asked quietly as she let her eyes wander over the proud aristocratic features.

'Yes, I am a true Spaniard, my little English *infanta*,' he said softly. 'I have the fire of this savage heritage in my veins. True Spain still consists of wild, untamed landscapes, snow-white horses and black bulls. It is not always kind or...comfortable.'

'I think I had begun to know that,' she said ruefully.

'It is not the place for a little English girl with silver hair and eyes like bottomless pools.' His voice made love to her and in spite of herself she felt her bones turn liquid. 'There are no knights in shining armour here to rescue the English maiden in her pleasant green countryside.'

'Just knights in black velvet?'

He looked puzzled for a moment and then laughed softly, but his eyes gleamed oddly as they narrowed on her face. 'You think I am a knight?' he asked quietly. 'A kind, good man who fights the dragons?' There was something in his voice now, a hardness, almost a rawness, that stopped her from replying. 'Oh, *pequeña*, what an innocent you are.'

The arrival of Teresa to clear their plates prevented her from replying and as she ate the dessert of sliced bananas topped with nuts, raspberries and fresh cream she reflected that she wouldn't have known what to say anyway. The good food, helped by two glasses of chilled white wine and coffee liberally laced with brandy and cream, restored her to something near her normal self but she still had the strangest feeling she was on a different planet.

'We will sit on the terrace and finish our coffee.' She looked up, startled, to find Francisco's eyes on her face as he gestured for Teresa to pick up the silver tray and follow them. As she went to reach for her crutches he was there before her, bending down and lifting her into his arms before she had time to protest. 'You are as light as a feather,' he said softly as he strode out through the huge French doors at the far end of the room and on to an enormous stone-tiled terrace that ran the whole length of the back of the house, winding into the distance in the darkness. She was rigid in his arms, fighting the impulse to wind her arms more tightly round his neck and feel the black crispness of his hair beneath her fingers as she pulled his head down to ask for his lips.

I just don't believe this is happening to me, she thought wildly as he placed her carefully in a long swinging hammock, one of many that were scattered along the terrace along with a profusion of easy-chairs and tables in weathered cane vying with sweet-smelling potted shrubs, bright-coloured geraniums, lemon-scented verbenas and a host of other trailing plants in terracotta pots.

'You can relax, Lorne, I am not going to ravish you.' His voice was cold as he seated himself opposite her and she realised he had misunderstood her stiffness as fright. 'You are quite safe.'

'Yes, I know.' Her feelings were so confused, so bewildered that for a moment she felt a stab of anger at the perpetrator which was reflected in her voice as she answered him. He eyed her tightly for a moment and then shook his head slowly as he sighed softly.

'This is all a dream, it has to be.'

'What?' His voice had been so low that she hadn't heard him clearly.

'No matter.' He stretched out his long legs for a moment and then poured out two cups of fresh coffee from the tray Teresa had placed at his elbow. The night was hot and full of spiced scents, not a breath of wind stirring the plants and shrubs in the scented darkness.

'I have to go to Geneva tomorrow.' She stared at him in surprise as he spoke but he was looking beyond her into the darkness, his hard face taut and expressionless.

'Do you?' She paused uncertainly. 'Well, if I don't see you again thank you very much for all you've done and——'

'I do not think it is advisable for you to travel with your ankle in such a condition.' He still didn't look at her. 'I would like to suggest that you stay here for a few days while I am gone. My presence may have worried you but as that will not be a consideration...'

'Stay here?' At the sound of her whispered gasp he turned to face her, a kind of caustic humour turning his eyes icy.

'Is that too terrible to contemplate?'

'No, of course not.' She found herself babbling but she couldn't help it. 'But you've been so kind already, there's really no need.'

'Is that a yes or a no?'

As she stared into the handsome bronzed face a few inches from her own it came to her suddenly that she *wanted* to stay, *wanted* to hold on to the link that kept her in his orbit at least for a little while longer. It was madness, she acknowledged painfully; all he had done since he first saw her was to emphasise how young and foolish he found her, but...she wanted to stay. This was probably going to be one of the biggest mistakes in her life, relegating the episode with Sancho and Janie to a mere hiccup in comparison, but she wanted to find out more about this dark, cold, passionate stranger.

'It's a yes, and I really do appreciate all you've done.'

'All I have done?' He stared at her through the dusky perfumed air. 'Frightened you half to death after you had placed yourself in my care?' White teeth flashed in a wry smile in the darkness of his face. 'This is the English good manners?' She sensed that some tautness had left his body but couldn't understand why. Perhaps she had imagined it; she wouldn't be surprised what she imagined in this enchanted corner of the world. She certainly didn't recognise herself any more but there was something wonderfully restful in letting someone else take over and take the responsibility from her shoulders, just for a few days. It was a luxury she wasn't used to, she reflected wryly.

'I will inform Alfonso that you are my guest until I return from Geneva.' His voice was cool and expressionless and she wondered if she

should have refused the invitation to stay.
Perhaps that had been what he expected?
Especially as it was only this peculiar sense of
Spanish hospitality that had forced him to make
the offer. 'He will also make arrangements for
an X-ray and so on.'

'Thank you.' Her voice was small.

As she lay in bed later that night her mind
wandered back and forth over the last twenty-
four hours, especially the last two or three. They
had continued to sit on the veranda for another
hour and Francisco had been the perfect host,
charming, courteous and very correct. As she
thought back on their conversation she realised
he had drawn out almost the whole of her life
history, such as it was, but had parried all her
attempts to question him with such consummate
ease that it was only now she realised she knew
absolutely nothing about him.

He had carried her up to her room, setting her
down outside the door and motioning Teresa,
who had followed with the crutches, back downstairs. 'Goodnight, *pequeña*.' His voice had been
very soft and deep and as a flush of pink had
stained her cheeks he had touched their softness
with his hands, cupping her face gently in his
large palms. It had been as though he was hyp-
notised by her mouth as he'd brushed her lips
with his own, but the kiss had not deepened;
indeed he had moved away swiftly as though regretting touching her at all. The shaft of disappointment she had felt then pierced her again as
she remembered.

After tossing and turning for another full hour she gave up all thought of sleep. Her ankle was hurting badly again but it was this strange feeling of restless excitement that was keeping her wide awake. She hobbled over to the small balcony outside her full-length windows, which were open to the warm night air, the whisper-thin night-dress that she had found on the bed after returning to the room after dinner clinging to the lines of her body.

Beyond the darkness she knew there was terrace upon terrace stretching away from the house, planted with cypress, myrtle and oleanders and all manner of scented and flowering shrubs. Francisco had described it all to her as they had sat on the veranda, his voice low and melodious and his eyes warm when they rested on her listening face.

As she sat on one of the cushioned chairs in the thick fragrant darkness she felt her tired limbs slowly begin to relax, the pain in her ankle turning into a dull ache and her mind going into a semi-doze as the quietness took over. She was just thinking of returning to bed when she heard Alfonso's voice. 'Señor de Vega?'

'*Sí, Alfonso*?' There was a movement from the veranda, which she realised must be directly below her balcony, and then Alfonso's quiet voice spoke again, a faint note of apprehension in the careful tones along with a definite note of apologetic concern. As the conversation progressed she sensed that Alfonso was worried about something and somehow, although it was ridiculous and probably pure imagination, she felt it concerned her in some way. After some moments Francisco's voice cut in abruptly, a deep coldness in its depths chilling her blood, and then she heard the two men move through the French doors into the house and the sound of their voices was lost. She sat for some minutes more wondering what it had all been about and then hobbled back to bed, climbing under the cool cotton sheets and falling asleep as soon as her head touched the pillow.

'*Señorita*?' Next morning Lorne awoke to Teresa's gentle hand on her shoulder as Benita beamed good morning by her side, holding a silver tray from which the aroma of fresh coffee rose tantalisingly. 'The *señor* thought you like the breakfast here—*sí*? And then you up——' Teresa waved her hands upwards graphically '—and he speak with you before he go away?'

'Yes, that's fine, thank you.' As she struggled up in bed a sharp pain in her ankle reminded her to be careful and, seeing her wince, Benita pointed to two small white pills on the tray.

'Señor de Vega say you have these after you eat, *señorita*.'

'Thank you.' When the two maids had left after placing the tray on her lap Lorne gazed down on the vast quantity of food. Toasted rolls with various preserves, fresh croissants and a selection of ripe fruit, sliced and ready to eat, and what looked like an omelette with rolled slices of pink ham on another plate along with a pot of coffee and fresh orange juice. She felt a wry smile touch her lips. If she ate even a quarter of this she would never be able to get out of bed!

Francisco was waiting for her in the huge marble hall as she negotiated the stairs half an hour later, and as he rose from his seat, thrusting some papers that he had been studying into a black leather briefcase at her approach, she felt her stomach lurch violently again. He was dressed in a light grey suit and blue silk shirt, the darkness of his skin and the way the lightweight material accentuated his broad shoulders and big frame making him seem very foreign.

'Good morning, Lorne.' The warm darkness in his eyes belied the distant voice. 'You slept well?'

'Eventually.' She smiled carefully. He was too attractive for his own good, or certainly for *her* good!

'The ankle will be more comfortable today,' he said in the impersonal tones of a doctor, 'and Alfonso will drive you to the hospital after lunch. The arrangements have been made.'

'Thank you.''

'Teresa and Benita will bring you a selection of my sister's clothes; please feel free to wear what you wish. I would have suggested that you shop for some suitable clothing but your ankle needs rest.'

She stared at him in consternation. He seemed so cold and formal this morning, so distant and unapproachable; did he really think she would allow him to buy her clothes in addition to everything else he had done for her? She suddenly felt acutely uncomfortable. She shouldn't be here. Shouldn't be letting a virtual stranger do so much. He would think she was taking advantage, think——

'Is there anything you wish to ask before I leave? Anything you wish to say?'

She felt a moment of pure panic at the thought of him leaving and then gave herself a firm mental shake. She'd known him less than twenty-four hours, for goodness' sake. The feeling that her security and safety were going with him was quite ridiculous.

'Only... thank you.' Her grey eyes were huge in the delicate softness of her face and as his gaze wandered over her pale skin he stiffened, his eyes dark and glittering and his face grim as he looked down at her.

'I must be mad.' As he bent towards her he took her arms in his hands, pulling her against him almost violently as though he was angry at something. But his kiss was warm, warm and deep and sensual, and she wanted it to go on forever. She was free again in a moment but not before she had felt the shudder that ran through his body and as he turned away she saw that his face was rigid with control.

'I shall be gone a few days.' He picked up the briefcase and walked to the front door without looking at her again and she stood where he had left her, swaying slightly, her thoughts in turmoil. 'If you wish to call anyone, go anywhere, you only have to ask Alfonso, you understand?'

He turned at the door with a brief smile and then was gone, with only the lingering aroma of expensive aftershave to convince her he had been there at all.

The hospital visit confirmed Francisco's diagnosis and that night she slept deeply, tired and exhausted from the combination of the long, hot journey in the heat of the day, the constant ache in her ankle and the few hours' sleep she had had the night before.

The next three days passed slowly. She was aware that Francisco telephoned his home each night but when Alfonso took the call he never spoke in English and she had no idea whether Francisco asked after her at all. The manservant seemed to dislike her; he rarely spoke unless it was absolutely necessary and his eyes were cold and hard if she ever caught his glance. Benita and Teresa were different—they were quite friendly—but their lack of English and her total ignorance of Spanish made communication difficult. Nevertheless, by the afternoon of the third day the little maids were chatting more freely to her and it was then she learnt a little more about the master of Silveria, as the massive estate was called.

She had spent the morning exploring the house and the grounds close by, the crutches giving her some freedom of movement now she was used to manipulating them, and after a light lunch had fallen asleep in one of the swinging hammocks on the veranda. When Benita awoke her about four with a glass of iced lemonade Lorne gestured for her to be seated at her side for a moment and the little maid smilingly obliged.

'This is a gorgeous place to live,' Lorne said quietly as her eyes ran over the shadow-blotched veranda sheltered from the fierce sun by its wooden roof and the profusion of trailing plants. 'How long have you worked here?'

'So many years, *señorita*.' Benita held up eight fingers. 'But Teresa, she born here. Alfonso is her father.'

'Is he?' Lorne thought about the dour-faced Alfonso and bright-eyed Teresa and, try as she might, could find no family resemblance.

'I come when Teresa's mother die. To help.' Lorne nodded to show that she understood. 'Is very sad time.' Benita shook her head slowly. 'The *señor*, we all worried for him.'

'You were worried for him because Teresa's mother died?' Lorne asked in surprise.

'No, no.' Benita shook her head again. 'They all die.'

'Who?' Lorne felt she was losing her grasp of the conversation rapidly.

'The *señor*'s mother, his brother, all of them.'

'You are talking too much, Benita.' As the cold voice interrupted them Lorne turned her head quickly to see Alfonso standing in the doorway, his face glowering. He had obviously heard their conversation and thoroughly disapproved; the rebuke in English had been for her benefit, she surmised. Benita disappeared in a second, her cheeks red, and as Alfonso made to follow her Lorne called to him, her voice hesitant.

'Alfonso?'

He turned to face her again, his brown eyes veiled. '*Sí, señorita*?'

'What did she mean, they all died? Who died and how?'

'Is not for me to say, *señorita*.' The old face was expressionless but the condemnation at her enquiry was obvious.

'Please, Alfonso.' As he turned away again she spoke quickly. 'I'm not just being nosy, I want to understand...' She had almost added Francisco's name, that she wanted to understand him, but stopped herself just in time.

Alfonso turned to face her again, his dark eyes searching her features intently as though he wanted to look into her mind. 'He has had enough heartache, *señorita*,' he said quietly after a time. 'I do not want him to be hurt any more.'

'No, I'm sure you don't.' She stopped abruptly. She didn't understand any of this. 'But I might be able to help——'

'No, *señorita*!' Alfonso took a pace towards her, his face fierce with dislike, and then, as if suddenly remembering his place, he stepped backwards, his eyes heavy. 'It would be best for you to go, to go now, *señorita*. I have money, I can help you.'

'I can't just leave.' She stared aghast at the old man's face and noticed there was real desperation in the brown eyes. 'Perhaps if you could explain...?'

He stared at her for another long moment and then sighed angrily, muttering a phrase under his breath that was more suited to the less salubrious regions of Madrid, before moving closer to her side and beginning to speak in rapid broken English. 'There was an accident, two years after Señor Rodrigo, the *señor*'s father, died. Señor Francisco's mother, his brother and his family and several of the servants died. That is all.'

'That's all?' She stared at him in horror. 'Where did it happen, *what* happened?' Alfonso's wife had died in that accident; how could he say 'That is all'?

'On the family yacht, an explosion.' The brown eyes were disturbingly hostile.

'And Francisco wasn't there?'

The brown eyes shifted from hers. 'No.' The word was flat. 'The *señor* was . . . elsewhere.'

'I see.' It was a lie; she didn't see at all. There was something more, something Alfonso wasn't telling her.

'The *señor*——' Alfonso shrugged Latin-style '—it was devastating for him, but these things happen. It is life.' He clearly didn't intend to say another word as he gave her one last long look and disappeared back into the house. Lorne sank back on to the hammock pillows with a frown wrinkling her smooth brow.

'Curiouser and curiouser'. But she wasn't Alice and this was no wonderland. Her eyes wandered round her magnificent surroundings. Or perhaps it was. One thing was certain, she didn't fit in here at all, and Alfonso's attitude had only intensified the unease she had been feeling for the last three days.

There was barely a moment when she hadn't allowed thoughts of Francisco's dark face and long, lean body to creep into her consciousness. She had never felt like this before about a man and it frightened her. She had to leave, soon.

The tightness the realisation brought to her throat grew until it was a painful knot. The physical attraction she felt for Francisco de Vega was dangerous and lethal and its power had even reached out over the miles separating them. He thought she was young and foolish, but she was not so young or foolish that she didn't recognise his sensual expertise when he had made love to her. He must have had women, lots of women, a man like him would have no difficulty in getting any female he wanted, and those few minutes in his arms had told her that beneath the cold, austere exterior ran pure fire. And fire could be deadly, withering everything in its path.

As soon as he returned and she had thanked him for the brief refuge she would leave. She would manage with her ankle somehow, she wouldn't let him do another thing for her, because suddenly Francisco, the mystery she sensed in this place, Alfonso's hostility and the sheer grandeur of her surroundings was all too much. She wanted to go home.

# CHAPTER FOUR

LORNE heard his voice first, deep and rich and unmistakably his as he talked to someone in the house, and then he was walking through the French doors on to the veranda where she was sitting enjoying the warm dusk before dinner. Her heart was pounding so hard that she barely heard his greeting but she must have mumbled something in reply because the next moment he had seated himself beside her on the cane settee, stretching out his long legs with a tired sigh before turning to face her. 'How is my stray lamb?' he asked mockingly.

It was amazing that with the blood surging through her veins in a flood of excitement and her flesh quivering at his nearness that one sentence should make her want to hit him, hard! She didn't want him to see her as a stray lamb, she wanted . . . She didn't know what she wanted.

It took considerable effort to keep her voice cool and low but she managed it, even forcing a light smile to her lips as she looked into the hard, glittering black eyes, her body acutely aware of the feel of his thigh against hers on the narrow seat. 'The ankle is much better, thank you,' she said quietly. 'How was your trip?'

'Tiring.' Benita came scurrying out of the house, carrying a tray holding a bottle of wine and two glasses which she put on a low table at their feet. As Francisco inclined his head towards the little maid with a smile of thanks she looked startled for a brief moment, turned a vivid shade of red and scampered back through the open doors even faster than she had arrived.

'She's very in awe of you.' Lorne spoke her thoughts out loud before she had time to think.

'*Sí*.' There was satisfaction in the word. 'She can be a little capricious, that one; it is good for her to learn discipline. I will not tolerate an attitude of waywardness—she knows this.'

She had looked forward to him coming home, far more than she had admitted to herself, she acknowledged painfully, but the emotion that was now filling her body with tightness was burning anger. What was the matter with him? she asked herself furiously. First that patronisingly superior comment to her and then this condescending, haughty attitude to little Benita. Whoever he had been with on this business trip had fed his ego to bursting-point!

'Have I said something wrong?' She hadn't realised she was glaring quite so ferociously but now, as his lazy voice interrupted her thoughts, she saw that there was black humour in his narrowed jet eyes. 'You disagree with control and restraint?'

'Not in the training of a dog, no.' For all her blonde fragility she had never yet refused a challenge.

'Ah, I see.' He bent forward and poured two glasses of sparkling white wine and didn't speak again until he had handed her hers. 'You think I am too authoritative perhaps, too harsh?'

'Do you really want me to answer that,' she asked seriously as her great grey eyes searched his dark face, 'or is it one of those questions where only a certain answer will do?'

He stared at her for a long silent moment, his eyes locked on to hers with such intensity that the world seemed to freeze around them, and then he surprised her totally by laughing softly as his features relaxed slightly. 'I was right about you, *infanta*,' he murmured quietly as his mouth closed over hers, hot and stunningly sweet. 'The man who awakens the slumbering beauty within will have his hands full.'

Although the kiss had only lasted a moment she felt the warmth of it for long minutes afterwards, hating the desire he could ignite so casually even as the thrills of excitement continued to trickle down her spine. As they sat there in the scented air she noticed after a time that he was keeping the conversation easy and general with a smooth polish that sat comfortably on him, his arrogance sophisticated and cool. This wasn't the real man. The thought flashed into her consciousness with devastating surety. He was playing a game he had probably perfected years ago, hiding his thoughts and emotions behind an impenetrable wall of social elegance. But why? She found her mind was working on a different plane altogether even as she responded to the niceties of social intercourse. Why did he feel such a need to hide so rigidly behind a mask?

'Shall we?' As Francisco took her arm to lead her through to the dining-room she felt his touch burn through the thin fabric of her dress and in spite of herself she almost stumbled. This was ridiculous. She had had a week to prepare herself for his return; she wouldn't let herself be knocked off balance by what was a pure animal reaction to his overpowering male attractiveness.

Her smile was brittle and her eyes shadowed as she took her place at the table, and as Benita and Teresa served the first course her resolve strengthened. She would tell him, as soon as a suitable opportunity presented itself, that she was well enough to leave. She could just about manage without the crutches now if she was careful, besides which he was probably expecting her to leave now that he was back. Anyway...she couldn't stay, she just couldn't.

'Lorne?' She realised he had been speaking and she hadn't heard a word, and as she raised her eyes to his she saw the phantom of a smile touch the black eyes. 'Is it thoughts of a particular...friend that is putting that expression on your face?'

'A friend?' she asked blankly.

'I was wondering if there was anyone in England who is waiting for you,' he said smoothly. 'A boyfriend, perhaps?'

'No.' She had answered before she had had time to think and could have kicked herself immediately the denial was voiced. An answer in the affirmative would have been some protection against... Against what? she asked herself silently. He hadn't exactly forced himself on her, had he? In fact that episode in the bedroom had indicated how easy he had found it to walk away from her, whereas she——

'I am surprised.' His voice was quiet now with something in its depths she couldn't quite place.

'Remember the friends I came to Spain with? Well, one of them was a boyfriend,' she said quickly as something flickered in the air between them that caused her cheeks to flush. 'There were four of us, two twosomes,' she continued stumblingly, 'but it didn't work out and so...'

'I see.' If she had been looking at him instead of at her plate she would have seen the dark face tighten but his voice was quite expressionless when he next spoke. 'And this caused you pain?'

'At the time,' she admitted honestly, 'but I think it was hurt pride more than anything else. Sancho——'

'Sancho?' Now the sharpness in his tone brought her eyes shooting up to meet his. 'This boy you came here with, he was Spanish?' She nodded silently. 'And he was happy for you to disappear by yourself in a strange country with no visible means of protection?' She didn't quite know how to answer. The blackness in his face was tangible.

'Not exactly.' She lowered her gaze and took a sip of wine as Teresa cleared their plates away and Benita placed several covered dishes on the table along with clean crockery, and then pro- ceeded to serve them both.

When the two maids had disappeared again he spoke her name in a voice which was quiet but vibrated with command. 'Lorne?' She looked at him slowly. 'You will tell me the circumstances of your being alone in my country and I want *all* of it this time, do you understand me?'

She opened her mouth to argue and then closed it again quickly. There was something in the hard, ruthless face that prompted caution.

'Well, it's more or less as I told you,' she began weakly. 'I came here with Sancho and two other friends. He was going to show me—us—his country and then we were maybe going to continue on around Europe for a few months, getting work where we could to pay our way, but then...'

As she continued with her tale the dark face was quite expressionless, even when she related the humiliating episode of finding Sancho and Janie together, and after she had finished he remained quite still for a moment before leaning forward and looking at her with an expression that suddenly drew back the veil and blazed with hot fury.

'So to punish this Sancho after finding him *in flagrante delicto* you decided to place yourself in as vulnerable a position as you could? If you had been raped or murdered he was supposed to feel extreme and undying guilt, is that it?'

'No!' She glared at him furiously. 'Of course that's not it and don't put words in my mouth either!'

'Put words in your mouth?' He settled back in his chair as he spoke and took a long, slow sip of wine as he eyed her through narrowed, devastingly cold eyes. 'Any words I could put in your mouth could only be an improvement, Lorne. Do you seriously mean to tell me that you decided to take off by yourself in spite of being woefully unprepared just to prove a point? I really cannot believe that a woman of your age and intelligence could be so criminally stupid.'

It was the first time he had acknowledged both her age and intellect but she was too angry to notice. A tiny part of her mind, ruthlessly ignored, was accepting the grain of truth in his words but as she rose from the table to glare across at him, her grey eyes shooting daggers, everything in her rose to meet his arrogance. 'And just who do you think you are, Francisco de Vega?' she hissed furiously. 'So right, so clever, I don't suppose you were ever young and did something you hadn't thought out thoroughly first, did you? You must have been the most obnoxious child ever born because you are certainly the most obnoxious man!'

'Sit down, Lorne.' His voice was perfectly controlled and intensely irritating. 'You are making a spectacle of yourself.'

'Am I indeed?' She was fighting back tears now and desperate that he didn't know. 'Well, that's about what you'd expect from such a person as me, isn't it? You aren't normal, Francisco, you really aren't.'

'Maybe not,' he agreed tightly as she still stood, rigid and stiff with her hands clenched into fists by her side, glaring across at him. 'But, normal or not, if you don't sit down within the next two seconds I shall come over there and make you. I will not have such an occurrence in front of my staff.'

He meant it; she could tell from the almost savage control that had darkened the handsome face into pure granite.

'I hate you.' As she sank back into her seat the spasm of pain that twisted his face for a brief moment was lost on her. 'You've made all this out to be my fault and it wasn't like that, it wasn't like that at all.'

There was total silence between them for painful minutes as Lorne kept her eyes fastened on her plate, and then as he spoke her name in a soft voice her face rose instinctively to his. 'You are wrong on several counts, *infanta*,' he said quietly as their eyes locked. 'I have done many things which with hindsight I regret and one thing in particular which far outweighs your crime. The only person you put at risk in your little display of defiance was yourself, after all.' There was something working in his face, something dark and terrifying that stilled her tongue more completely than his anger could have done and her eyes were huge as they remained fixed on his. 'And I do not blame you altogether for this situation in which you find yourself. You were unwise and impulsive but this Sancho...' His lip curled away from his teeth as his eyes sparked light. 'I would like to be alone with such a man for five minutes. To let you down so badly and then allow you to venture on alone...' He shook his head slowly. 'He could never have been right for you, do you see this?'

She did, she had known it all along really, but just at the moment, for some perverse reason she couldn't have explained even to herself, she was incapable of admitting it.

As she stared at him without answering his fingers tightened on the stem of his wine glass, belying the relaxed posture, and just for a moment, a swift and stunning moment, she glimpsed the inner man before his eyes were veiled. The dark force, the intensity of emotion was vital, and she took a gulp of her own drink to calm suddenly tight nerves. She didn't understand this, *him*, and was more sure than ever that she didn't want to. She had made up her mind to go days ago, and from what had transpired it would seem he would be glad to see the back of such a silly and impulsive creature, so she would tell him *now*. It would be a relief to both of them. The little kick her heart gave was just nerves, she assured herself quickly, and quite understandable in the circumstances.

'Lorne, I fear the memories you will carry home of my beautiful country will not be happy ones, *sí*?'

The total change in conversation threw her.

'Sorry?' She swallowed tightly.

His eyes were steady on hers, probing, but quite cool now, all expression carefully banked. 'I feel responsible that it was my countrymen that have ruined your holiday here. First this Sancho person——' the thread of disdain couldn't be hidden '—and then the boys who frightened you so badly. You must not think that these people are indicative of what is average.'

'No,' she agreed faintly, opening her mouth to say more and then shutting it abruptly. 'No...'

'I would like to make amends in a small way, if you would allow me to do so?' the expressionless voice asked quietly.

'You would?' For an awful moment she thought he was going to offer her money.

'Your ankle should be sufficiently recovered in a few more days for a little sightseeing. Would you do me the honour of allowing me to show you a little of my country? There is much beauty here and much hospitality. I do not wish your reminiscences in the future to be tainted, you understand?'

Oh, yes, she understood, she thought painfully. He was fiercely, unashamedly proud of his Spanish heritage and if she recounted the incident on the road along with Sancho's duplicity it wouldn't sound too good, would it? And so he would sacrifice a few days of his life in order to show this nuisance of a stray the lighter side of Spain. Well, he needn't bother! The pain his words had caused was a thick strong thing in her chest. 'There's no need for that,' she said quickly. 'I know you're very busy and——'

'I put that very clumsily.' As he reached across and took her hand she knew he had read her mind again. 'I make this invitation because I wish to be with you, *infanta*. Soon you will be back in your own country and this will merely be a dream. I would like it to be a good one.'

The warmth in his dark face was genuine, it had to be, she told herself fiercely, and although the thrill that shot unbidden through her body was a warning she knew she was going to ignore it. She wanted a few days with him; that wouldn't hurt anyone, would it? she argued silently, although the knowledge that he could smash all her resolutions with just a few kind words and a smile after practically accusing her of who knew what was...worrying. Her brain was telling her to leave now, while there was still time to walk away with no involvement, no ties, but her heart was urging her to take the promise of this brief interlude and make the most of every moment.

'Thank you.' The hesitation in her voice was reflected in her face and for a fleeting moment amusement lightened his classical features, causing the black eyes to soften and appear almost depthless. Her heart hammered against her chest wall again. He was such an enigma, this man. He spelt danger with a capital D. She should never have agreed to stay, she shouldn't——

'You will rest the ankle a little while longer and then we will explore together, *sí*?' His voice was light and pleasant; he had slotted back into the attentive-host mode, but it was far from re-assuring somehow. He was so complex, such a mystery, whereas she was an open book, she thought dismally, and just as uninteresting. He was an assured man of the world, fabulously wealthy, used, no doubt, to adoring women flocking round him at every turn—— Stop it, Lorne, she told herself savagely as she jabbed an inoffensive piece of meat with her fork, horrified at the way her mind was working. This was just a holiday and he wanted her to have some pleasant memories to take back to England. He had made that crystal-clear. And that was exactly how she was going to treat the next few days. And after that, home.

There were no awkward questions to spoil the rest of the meal but, try as she might, Lorne found the food was almost tasteless in her mouth. She had never considered herself highly strung, just the opposite, in fact. The blow of losing her dearly loved parents at such a tender age, the adjustments needed to integrate into Tom's family with the minimum of fuss added to a naturally independent and strong spirit had armed her well for the twists and turns of life, but this... This was something different. Somehow one glance from those ebony eyes reduced her to... A gibbering idiot, she told herself wryly as she searched for a suitable expression to cover her turmoil. And she didn't like it, not one little bit. And it had *got* to stop.

'The food has disagreed with you?' As the silky-smooth voice cut into her thoughts she caught the thread of caustic humour in its rich depths with a quick dart of resentment. He found all this amusing? She raised serious grey eyes to meet his mocking gaze. He found *her* amusing?

'I'm sorry?' She was pleased her voice was so cool.

'I was wondering if it was the food that has put such a ferocious expression on your face?' He eyed her laconically. 'Or maybe you are exercising the age-old right of your sex to sulk?'

'Wrong on both counts, as it happens,' she said lightly, forcing her eyes away from his with a strength of self-will she'd never known she had. 'I'm just a little tired, that's all. The last few weeks have been difficult and I suppose it's all caught up with me now I'm so relaxed.' And put that in your pipe and smoke it, she thought childishly and with a venom that surprised her. Relaxed? She had never been less relaxed in her life!

'But this is very good.' The black eyes were dancing with something she didn't care to define. 'The healing processes are greatly accelerated when the mind is calm and at peace. We will soon have you quite recovered.'

'Yes.' She smiled flatly. 'Well, if you'll excuse me, I think I'll go to bed.'

'Of course.' He rose immediately to bring her crutches to her side but just as he reached her she swayed slightly as she stood on one foot and in the same instant that his hand reached out to steady her she instinctively jerked to avoid his touch. She knew a moment's panic as she felt herself falling and then he had caught her, his hands strong and firm on her waist as they pulled her into his rock-hard body.

'Lorne . . .' She could have avoided his mouth, she acknowledged to herself even as her lips opened beneath his, but it would have been as impossible as trying to stop breathing. She had been longing, *aching*, for the feel of him and the need was overpoweringly potent. He was devouring her mouth almost helplessly, all control gone, and with a thrill of horror she found herself responding with a passion that matched his, utterly wanton as she strained closer to him, the taste and smell of his maleness all-encompassing.

The embrace could only have lasted a few seconds but as he pushed her from him, almost violently, her whole body was on fire and she would have fallen again if his hands hadn't kept their grip on her arms as he held her firmly at arm's length.

'Francisco?' She knew she was staring up at him with a stupid dazed expression on her face but for the life of her she couldn't hide the confusion and painful puzzlement that was spearing through her at the frightening blackness of his face. He looked... He looked as though he hated her.

'Go to bed, Lorne.' His voice was at variance with the savage emotion etched into the coldly handsome features. It was almost mild in its lack of expression.

'But I don't understand. What's wrong...?'

He bent down in one swift movement and placed the crutches in her arms, his hands rough and jerky. 'There is nothing wrong,' he said coldly. 'You wanted to go to bed, so go.' It was calculated cruelty and all the more devastating for its unexpectedness.

As he stepped back a pace, his body rigid and taut and his eyes blank, she felt a hot biting retort spring through the burning humiliation and pain but in the same breath an awareness, a sixth sense that was stronger than the normal human reaction of revenge and retaliation, told her this was another disguise, another mask. He was hurting. Why, how, she didn't know, but he *was* hurting, and badly. So badly that it melted her desire for a counter-blow. And the sudden longing to comfort him, the fierceness of her desire to offer solace and succour frightened her more than all that had gone before.

# CHAPTER FIVE

'I THOUGHT I would find you here.'

As Lorne glanced up from the English magazine she was reading, shading her eyes against the brilliance of the blue sky overhead which gave the air a piercing quality of light, she smiled carefully. The last ten days since Francisco's return had been an education on how to hide one's feelings. She didn't like it, she even despised herself a little for taking the easy way out, but when on the morning after his reappearance he had entered the large breakfast-room with a polite nod and a courteous enquiry after her health she had felt as though some momentous catastrophy had been averted, and it had seemed easier to pretend that she was just a normal house guest enjoying a short holiday for a while.

'It's so pretty.' She repeated the congenial smile.

'Yes, it is.' As he sat down beside her on one of the generously upholstered sun-loungers scattered by the huge kidney-shaped swimming-pool she felt her stomach muscles contract violently. He had obviously come prepared to swim, his well-muscled brown body naked except for a pair of brief black swimming-trunks that accentuated a certain part of his anatomy far more expertly

than any nudity could have done, and when this
was combined with the broad masculine
shoulders and tight black curly hair covering his
chest he looked...delicious. Delicious and
dangerously tempting as all forbidden fruit was.
But she wasn't going to think along those lines!
She gave a mental nod. He had made it clear over
the last week or so, with his cool civility and
formal manners, that the brief physical attraction he had felt for her had died a swift death.
And she was glad! The sick feeling in her stomach
reproached the lie. She was, *she was*. He was
ruthless, cold and hard and it would be sheer
suicide to harbour any romantic notions about
this man, as crazy as falling for an inexorable
robot.

'My father had the pool built for my mother
when she first came here,' Francisco continued
quietly as he leant back lazily against the lounger
with his hands behind his head and his eyes shut
against the bright afternoon light, 'and he knew
it was imperative to make the surroundings as
beautiful as possible. My mother had a great appreciation of anything lovely.'

Lorne glanced round the exquisitely land-
scaped gardens surrounding the pool area, where
almond, orange and lemon trees vied with purple
and pink bougainvillaea, brightly coloured geraniums and pelargoniums and lemon-scented
verbena and to the rear of it all a mass of wonderfully perfumed gorse, lavender and thyme.
The brilliantly blue sky overhead, the rich colours
of the vegetation complementing the tiny walls

of blindingly white stone and the floor tiles of a deep satisfying red all merged together into a glorious whole that was quite stunning. 'She must have loved it here,' she said slowly.

'Yes, she did.' He rose suddenly as though something had disturbed him. 'Are you swimming?'

'I went in earlier.' She kept her eyes fixed on his face determinedly; that near-naked body was too close for comfort.

'It was a pity she didn't live longer to see her grandchildren playing at the water's edge in the warmth of long summer days,' he said flatly as though the previous conversation hadn't been broken.

'Yes…' There was a harsh rigidity in the proud face that warned her to say nothing of what Alfonso had told her about the terrible accident that had wiped out all his kith and kin. She searched desperately for a remark that would sound natural. 'My bother found it hard when my parents died. His children were very tiny then, twin girls of three months and two boys under three. He felt my mother especially had missed out on seeing them grow up; she loved children.'

Her voice seemed to bring him back from a long dark journey and as the black eyes focused on her again she was relieved to see the taut features relax a little. 'Yes.' He nodded distantly as the veiled look came over his face. 'Life is a cruel game at best.'

As he dived into the water she sank back against the soft cushions with her head spinning.

There was still something she didn't understand here, something deep, something Alfonso knew but had no intention of telling her. A thin trickle of something icy shivered down her spine. And that look on his face, it had been . . . terrifying.

'How's the ankle?' As he hauled himself out of the pool, brown skin gleaming with tiny diamond droplets of water that the sun picked out in glittering detail, she saw he was smiling, smiling and relaxed and cool as though their conversation had never been. And she *knew* it was feigned.

'Much better.' She glanced down at her foot, which was its own shape again. 'Just the odd twinge now and again, that's all. You were right, you said two or three weeks.'

'Time for that sightseeing I promised you.' He walked over to the lounger with the lithe animal grace that seemed peculiar to him and she forced herself to show no reaction as he lowered himself on to the sun-warmed cushions. His body was magnificent. She closed her eyes tightly for a split-second as she took a long, deep hidden breath. Very tanned, very strong, like an advertisement for the male sex in general. How many women had he had? The thought surprised her eyes into opening wide. Had she really just thought that? Oh, brother, she had to watch herself, she really did. 'Culture or sea and sand first?' the deep voice asked lazily after a while.

His smile was slightly crooked and for once the near-ebony eyes were crystal-clear and with a tiny dart of pleasure she realised he had let his guard down, that this was a brief glimpse of the real Francisco. The lop-sided smile made him look like a little boy somehow and that traitorous flood of emotion shivered down her spine again. Did he know just how appealing he looked, how very sensual the combination of little boy lost and man of the world was to the female heart? Probably. She forced herself to smile casually. *Very* probably.

'Oh, sea and sand, I think.'

'Good. First thing tomorrow then we make the start, *si*?'

She slept badly that night and was furious with herself when, in the very early hours of the morning, she woke with her mind in gear and her thoughts racing. And it was all about him. She pounded the hapless pillows with her fists in impotent rage. What was the matter with her, for goodness' sake? Just because he had been so natural, so warm, that last hour by the pool before dinner didn't mean a thing, not a thing! Look at the last ten days. At best he had treated her as a distant guest, at worst as something to be avoided at all costs. Where was her pride, for crying out loud? She would not, *would not* run when he crooked his little finger! And this ridiculous feeling that she was somehow special because he had relaxed enough to let her see a little of the real man, it was probably the best line in the world! That was it, it was just a line. But it wasn't. She closed her eyes as she pulled a pillow over her face in an effort to stop the tumbling thoughts. She knew it wasn't.

'I thought we had a date?' As the light touch on her arm brought her from a deep sleep she opened dazed eyes to find she was cuddling the pillow that had been on her head to her in much the same way as a child cuddled a teddy bear, and Francisco was standing at her side with a distinctly grim look on his dark face that softened at her immediate apology.

'I'm so sorry...' She kept the pillow where it was; suddenly the elegant silk nightshirt borrowed from his sister seemed woefully transparent. 'I must have slept through Benita's morning call. I didn't sleep very well—my ankle...' she improvised rapidly as she realised what she had said.

'It's troubling you?' He was immediately the doctor. 'You would like me to have a look at it?'

'No!' The retort was more instinctive than polite and she forced her voice down a note as she qualified her refusal. 'No, it's fine now, really. I probably just wasn't very tired. No exercise.' She wanted to brush the soft blonde waves that had fallen across her face and shoulders out of her eyes but for some reason she didn't dare move. There was a warmth, a dark heat in his eyes as he stood looking down at her that made her feel she should keep as still as she could.

'You look delicious.' He hardly seemed aware that he had spoken and she stared up at him mesmerised as he crouched down at her side, his face a breath away from hers. 'Quite ridiculously delicious.' The sudden sense of exhilaration faded as quickly as it had come as he stood up again almost immediately, his eyes hooded. 'Ten minutes, Miss Wilson, and then I come to dress you myself.' The brief smile was dismissive.

As the door closed behind him she took several long shuddering breaths before leaping out of bed and having the quickest shower of her life, leaving her wet hair to dry on her shoulders as she dressed quickly in white leggings and sleeveless top, leaving the room exactly nine minutes after he had entered it.

He was waiting for her in the breakfast-room hidden behind his newspaper with a cup of black coffee in front of him. 'Very nice.' His eyes wandered across her scrubbed face appreciatively. 'But you look about fifteen this morning. People will think I am—how do you say it?—cradle-snatching.' There was a darkness in the ebony eyes she couldn't quite fathom, a definite withdrawal.

'Does it matter what people say?' she asked brightly.

'Ah, I was forgetting you are the student,' he smiled slowly. 'The take it and leave it policy of the young, *si*?'

He was trying to put distance between them, she could feel it, introduce a barrier, and suddenly everything in her rebelled. 'I'm not a student, actually,' she said firmly as she plonked down determinedly into her seat and faced him square on. 'If you remember, I've just qualified and, as I said, I've been looking after myself for years. I've always found age is a state of mind rather than a biological fact and I had to mature pretty early when Mum and Dad died. I can't help it if I *look* younger than I am; it's a family trait.' She eyed him tightly. 'And I've no intention of apologising to you about it either.'

He stared at her for a long moment before disarming her totally by smiling very slowly. 'I do not doubt this for a minute.' He bowed his head in a little nod of acknowledgement. 'And you are quite right to reprimand such an ungallant remark. I stand corrected.' There was a wicked gleam of amusement in his eyes now as he picked up his coffee-cup; Teresa bustled into the room with fresh croissants warm from the oven to add to the vast array of food on the table. 'And I am beginning to realise that beneath that fragile exterior beats a heart of pure steel.'

'I didn't say that either.' Try as she might she couldn't stop the hot colour flooding into her cheeks. 'But I'm not some sort of empty-headed, helpless female who can't say boo to a goose.'

'No, I can see this,' he agreed gravely. 'Believe me, this I *can* see.'

'Right, then...' To cover her confusion she made a show of piling her plate with food only to find she had selected far too much.

'You are hungry this morning, *infanta*?' Francisco smiled smoothly. 'I can only admire such a healthy appetite.'

She took the silky tone at face value considering it was the only course open to her and smiled sweetly in reply. She would eat this plateful of food now if it killed her! It nearly did.

Half an hour later as she followed Francisco out to the beautifully streamlined Ferrari sitting patiently in the drive she felt she was almost waddling. 'This is a dream of a car.' She glanced at him as he took his place in the driving seat. 'It must be every man's ultimate goal to own one of these.'

'Possibly.' The jeans-clad legs slid under the steering-wheel with the ease of familiarity. 'This impresses you?' The black eyes were cynical and she felt the bubble of anger he always seemed to induce burst into life at the overt criticism. Of course the beautiful machine impressed her; it had been built for that purpose, hadn't it? If he expected her to pretend a sophistication she didn't have, and more to the point didn't want, he was going to be bitterly disappointed!

'Well, it knocks the pants off a number ten bus,' she said sardonically, her shaped eyebrows raised in an unmistakably mocking grimace, 'and Shanks's pony isn't in the running either.'

'Shanks's pony?' He turned to face her, sliding one arm along the back of her seat, so near that the thick sweep of his black eyelashes was incredibly fascinating. 'What does this animal have to do with my car?'

'Absolutely nothing,' she admitted with a smile. 'It's just an English expression; it means using your own two legs to get from A to B; something, I suspect, you've never had to do.'

'And you disapprove of this?' His eyes were piercingly intent now, their darkness seeming to draw her in until it was almost painful to hold his gaze. 'You think I have been spoilt, maybe?'

'You're putting words in my mouth again,' she said faintly as the intoxicatingly sensual aftershave he favoured had her senses racing into overdrive. It didn't help that the open-necked, short-sleeved silk shirt he wore so casually displayed his muscled chest and broad shoulders to such good effect either. 'I never said anything about your being spoilt.'

'Well, you would have been right if you had,' he said surprisingly as he lifted a lock of silver-blonde hair from her shoulders and let it fall fanwise back into place. 'I was a wild young man, wild and inexcusably selfish.' He was speaking in a flat monotone, his face composed and still except for his eyes which were deep black pools of pain. 'I thought the world belonged to me and that I only had to reach out to something to possess it. And then I learnt that everything in life has to be paid for although it is not always fair or just. Sometimes the innocent pay dues that are not their own.'

She sat absolutely still as she stared at his face, the warm, clear, perfumed air drifting into the open car windows from the beautifully tended bushes and flowers edging the immaculate drive and the dancing flickers of sunlight filtering down through the giant cedar tree under which the car was parked somehow grotesquely out of place when compared to the savage darkness that had shadowed his face in the last few seconds.

'Francisco?' She touched the edge of his sleeve hesitantly. 'What's wrong?'

'Wrong?' As his eyes focused on her again the metamorphosis that she had witnessed several times before happened again and she could have cried with frustration. The mask slipped back into place, the eyes veiled and closed against her, and once again he was the cool, cynical, sardonic man she had met on the road from Extremadura nearly three weeks before, quietly assured and arrogantly confident. 'Nothing is wrong, my sweet little *infanta*; what could be wrong with such a fortunate man as I?' He turned the key in the ignition as he spoke and immediately the powerful car purred into life. 'I am going to take you to my beach-house today,' he continued urbanely as he swung the car round in a semicircle and nosed it down the drive. 'It isn't too far away and the sand shelves very gently into the sea. I do not want you to put too much strain on those ligaments and tendons all at once.'

He had gone into doctor mode and she knew why—he had been in danger of letting her get too close. What was the matter with him? She slanted a quick glance at his handsome face under her eyelashes and saw it was aloof and cold. Damn, damn, damn...

After a few miles the changing beauty of her surroundings began to soothe her agitation. It was impossible not to respond with delight to the sugar-white houses tumbling down green pine-clad hills, the fields of almond, olive and citrus trees hidden either side of quiet lanes hedged with hibiscus and jacaranda, a quaint sixteenth-century church here and an ancient medieval hilltop fortress there. In one small sleepy village that they passed through she was thrilled to see an old priest in a dusty soutane standing under the stone archway leading to his church with two mules with wooden saddles on their broad backs and old straw hats on their nobbly heads through which long ears emerged in comical hauteur. In another they passed a young, black-haired girl filling a brown jug at a decayed fountain, her bare feet and long red skirt calling up a picture of an age long since dead.

It was just eleven o'clock when Francisco urged the sleek red car down a never-ending lane surrounded by fragrant almond groves and vineyards, on and on until with a suddenness that was breathtaking they emerged into a deep secluded bay set against a dramatic backdrop of pine- and juniper-clad hills and craggy mountains. As he brought the car to a halt just before the dazzling white beach strewn with huge rose-pink and mother-of-pearl shells she saw a sprawling, traditional-style whitewashed villa some way up a small incline overlooking the bay of crystal-clear turquoise water.

'It's . . .' For a moment she couldn't find words to describe such a paradise. 'It's——'

'Inconvenient,' Francisco finished drily, indicating the lack of road with a wave of his hand. 'The last part of this journey is by the Shanks's pony of which you talk. You did not know he would come in handy so soon? Take my hand, please; we do not wish for any more accidents.'

His hand was warm as it enclosed her small paw and for a moment she had the crazy impulse to turn and fling herself into his arms. It was the sort of thing she had felt more than once lately and as they walked towards the villa she cautioned herself silently. None of that, Lorne, none of that. It didn't help but then it hadn't before either.

'This is a lovely spot.' As they neared the wooden veranda that ran the length of the front of the house she made a pretence of bending down to tip the soft sand out of her old black pumps. His sister's shoes had been one thing she couldn't borrow, being at least three sizes too big. She had needed to do something to break the physical contact that was causing tiny flickers of sensation to curl along her arm in ever-increasing circles. 'Have you owned this place long?' she asked with studied casualness.

'My grandfather had it built over eighty years ago,' Francisco said smoothly as he leaned back against one of the wooden supports with his hands in his jeans pockets and his eyes narrowed into black slits. 'It's more or less unaltered inside, just simple furnishings in an old rustic style. Rosa and Josef, the caretakers, live here on a permanent basis and have done since they were married nearly forty years ago.'

'Oh.' As she tipped out the second shoe she straightened and joined him on the veranda, the wood warm and smooth under her bare feet. 'You just visit occasionally?'

'Normally.' He looked past her to the wide expanse of sea and sky. 'There was a time, eight years ago, when I came here to stay for six months. I was ... unwell.'

'Oh, I'm sorry.' Her brain worked feverishly even as she made her voice offhand and casual. That must have been about the time of his family's deaths. 'There's nothing like sea air for helping the body to recover, is there?' She forced all trace of her knowledge from her eyes even as her heart cried out to him in sympathy. He must have been devastated, utterly devastated.

'It wasn't a physical illness,' he said shortly, his terse tone indicating that the conversation was at an end. 'Come along, come and meet Rosa and Josef. They are a little deaf but otherwise quite robust.' His smile was definitely forced.

The small elderly Spanish couple turned out to be dear old souls who treated Francisco with a warmth that was obviously genuine and had none of the stiff formality of Alfonso's dealings with his master. Lorne felt a ridiculous but undeniable shaft of piercing envy at the way Francisco hugged Rosa close as he kissed the paper-thin lined cheek, his black eyes warm and tender for once and his face open and unguarded. 'Here is the visitor I promised.' He drew Lorne to his side and moved her forward. 'Lorne, meet Rosa and Josef.' Just for a split-second Lorne saw Rosa's small beady black eyes move swiftly to Francisco's face, her grey head slightly on one side like an enquiring little pert robin, and then she was enfolded in the small Spanish woman's lavender-scented embrace.

'It is a long time since the *señor* has brought anyone to see us,' Rosa said softly in broken English. 'Far, far too long. I am very pleased to make your acquaintance, Señorita Lorne.' For a moment Lorne had the strangest feeling sweep over her again, an instinctive suspicion that the warm greeting meant more than just the polite words in which it was voiced. She shook the thought away immediately, annoyed with herself; she would be seeing goblins behind every doorpost if she wasn't careful and it wouldn't do, it wouldn't do at all.

'Thank you.' Once released she smiled into the bright little face that was on a level with hers. 'It's so beautiful here.'

It was. Francisco's idea of simple rustic furnishings was not exactly the norm, she reflected wryly as he led her through the small hall, ablaze with colour from the profusion of hanging plants covering all one wall, and into a large sun-drenched room that faced the sea, its white-painted walls alive with exquisite watercolours and the yellow and honey-coloured furnishings intensifying the impression of vibrant warmth and light.

As Francisco took her on a quick tour of the rest of the house she saw that every room was distinctive and interesting, rich stimulating colours combining with the elegant and dainty

furniture to give an overall effect that was
charming and yet curiously restful.

This must be a little oasis for him in the fast
world in which he moved, she thought percep-
tively, glancing at his dark face as they rejoined
Rosa and Josef in the downstairs room overlooking the sea. 'These paintings are really quite
lovely.' She glanced round the textured walls appreciatively. 'Are they all by the same artist?'

'Yes.' His voice was dismissive and he was
clearly not going to say any more but Rosa had
caught the question and now turned to her
quickly.

'The *señor*, he paint them.' She waved her
hands expansively to encompass the room. 'He
paint every one.'

'You did?' Her eyes were frankly incredulous.
'I didn't know you were an artist, that you could
paint like this.'

'I do not paint any more.' As the dark eyes
flashed over Rosa she melted quickly from the
room, Josef following her with a glance at
Francisco which seemed to hold an apology in
its depths.

Another secret? thought Lorne irritably. What
on earth was the matter with her knowing that
he painted? 'Why not?' It was not what he
wanted to hear but just at that moment in time
she didn't care. It had been his suggestion that
they come here and it wasn't in her nature to skirt
any issue; in fact she had been more careful in
the past weeks with this man than she had ever

been with anyone in her whole life. 'It seems like a terrible waste when you're so good.'

'You think so?' His voice was cold and tight and unmistakably insulting. 'But then I suspect you know very little about art.' The dark eyes were jet-black and ice-cold.

She raised her head slowly and met the hard gaze with her eyes level and firm and her mouth straight. 'I know what I like and to me that is all that matters,' she said slowly. Her chin rose a fraction higher as the piercing eyes held hers and she knew no power on earth could have stopped her from speaking the next words; he had had them coming since the first moment she had met him. 'And I have to say that for such a supposedly sophisticated and well-educated man your manners border on the pig-like.'

'I beg your pardon?' His eyes were diamond-hard and the big body had frozen into an almost comical attitude of disbelief.

'You heard me.' She wouldn't back down now, *couldn't*, but the trembling that was causing little ripples to spread weakly down her legs would soon communicate itself to her voice if she wasn't careful. 'You are rude and bad-mannered and arrogant. Perhaps I haven't been educated the way you've been and brought up in a big house with unlimited money but that doesn't mean my opinion is of no account. I've got my own thoughts and feelings about things and if they don't match with yours then that's just too bad. I'm not going to pussyfoot about being scared of my own shadow for you or anyone else. Now

I suppose you'll want to go straight back so I'll just say goodbye to Rosa and Josef.'

'Stand still!' The voice was like a whiplash and as he took the two steps that brought him straight in front of her she unconsciously raised her head in an attitude that was both instinctively defensive and curiously vulnerable as the pure slender line of her throat was exposed. 'How dare you suggest that I do not value you as a person?' His voice was shaking with rage. 'How dare you?'

'Because you don't.' The sudden confrontation had her stomach turning and her heart pounding but she knew that if she backed down now, let him browbeat her into saying that black was white and white was black, she would never have the courage to face this thing again. 'Right from the first second I met you you've had me feeling that I'm doing everything wrong, that there is something the matter with me. But there's not, *there's not*.' Her eyes were luminous with unshed tears and her mouth trembled in spite of her efforts to control it, but she still stood before him, small and waif-like, her hands clenched fists by her side and her back rigid with defiance. 'I know I'm not perfect, that I make mistakes, but I'm not stupid or——'

'But you are perfect, don't you see?' His voice was soft now and full of indescribable pain. 'Quite, quite perfect.' As he pulled her against him, holding her tight so that the thudding of his heart was echoed through hers, she felt a cold presentiment flicker down her spine, a frightening foreboding that chilled her blood in spite of the strength of his arms. There had been a hopelessness in his voice, an acceptance of something she couldn't quite determine, that was invincible. His will was iron-like, the intensity of his spirit untouchable. She could never reach him, never get through to the real man, she knew that now.

He held her close for one more instant and then pushed her away slightly, his voice still unsteady as he motioned to the sports bag he had brought with them. 'Go and change and we'll swim before lunch.'

'Francisco——'

'Please, Lorne.' He shut his eyes as he turned from her to stare out of the huge windows at the picturesque cove and glinting sea. 'No more.'

As she stumbled into the large cloakroom off the hall her legs buckled and she almost fell into the big basket seat in upholstered bamboo in the corner. She had just been through what was the worst moment of her adult life and she didn't have a clue what it had all been about. She brushed at her face ineffectually as hot, stinging tears seeped slowly down her cheeks. She wished she hadn't come to Spain, wished she'd never met him, wished she'd never been sucked into his dark, menacing orbit, because nothing, nothing would ever be the same again. In less than three weeks her world had been turned upside-down and she was still spinning crazily, hopelessly, out of control—but for how long? Her heart pounded violently. How long before she left this beautiful land, and him, forever?

## CHAPTER SIX

WHEN she emerged from the cloakroom ten
minutes later clad in a beautifully cut black
swimming-costume, her hair looped into a high
ponytail and her face washed clean of any trace
of tears, Lorne found Francisco waiting for her
in the hall, calm, contained and seemingly perfectly relaxed. But she had been expecting it this
time and the face that met his reflected his
coolness.

'Ready?' The black eyes flicked over her lazily,
their expression hidden behind congenial warmth.

'Yes.' She smiled back carefully. He was still
dressed in the jeans and black silk shirt he had
driven down in and she felt embarrassingly naked
in the silky scrap of expensive material from his
sister's amazing wardrobe.

The sand was hot beneath her feet as they left
the house and immediately the bright sun roasted
her skin with its powerful warmth as they wandered down to the water's edge. 'Come on.' As
he led her along the shoreline he took her hand
in a casual gesture that she knew meant nothing
but had her toes curling into the powdery sand
with a tiny thrill of pleasure. 'There is a small
inlet a little way ahead with a wonderfully shallow
slope into the water. The sea is always warm at
that point so the shock of the deeper water isn't

so bad.' He looked down at her, his eyes crinkled against the sun.

Part of her, a tiny separate part, was aware of the incongruity of the fact that here she was, ordinary little Lorne Wilson, wandering along a picture-postcard beach with one of the most handsomely enigmatic men she had ever seen in her life, and that included the Hollywood stars on the silver screen, when just a few weeks ago she had been slaving over her finals and unable to imagine a life that didn't include relentless study and persistent hard work.

Perhaps that was where she'd gone wrong, she thought suddenly. Maybe if she could look on this as a brief glimpse of how the other half lived, a pleasant interlude that would soon be forgotten once she was back in her own world, it wouldn't matter so much what he said or did. He had intimated virtually the same thing after all when he had suggested the sightseeing to improve the impression of his land she would take home with her. None of this mattered, not really... But it *did*, dammit, it did.

She felt the dark gaze on her face and glanced up to meet it. 'Somehow Catalina never looked like that in this swimming-costume,' he said slowly as the heat in his eyes became mirrored in her cheeks.

'Didn't she?' He had stopped and was looking down at her with glittering black eyes. 'Well, perhaps it's just because she's your sis——'

As his head lowered to hers her lips quivered and opened in mesmerised expectation, and her

name was a thick groan on his mouth as he pulled
her into his hard bulk. 'Lorne...' He traced the
outline of her lips, his tongue sensuous against
their soft fullness. 'This is crazy...' The kiss was
long and deep and satisfying and she didn't want
it to end even as she forced herself not to reach
up to him and obey the instinct that had her
yearning to pull his body even closer into hers,
to feel every line and contour of his male shape
against her softness. This didn't mean anything
to him beyond a brief affair, *couldn't* mean anything more to him. He had made that clear, if
not the reasons behind it. A brief affair? Her
thoughts mocked her. No, not even that. As he
raised his head again she saw that his mouth was
rueful. 'I think I need a swim.' She didn't understand what he meant at first but then, as he di-
vested himself of the jeans and shirt to reveal
brief black trunks beneath, his body told her
more eloquently than words that he was not
completely immune to her charms.

She tore her eyes away from the pure hard line
of his manhood with tremendous determination
and turned to face the open sea, her cheeks hot
and her heart pounding. He was so big, so
dangerous, so virile... She was playing with fire,
*she was*, so why couldn't she stop?

The water was beautifully warm at first but as
she waded deeper into the silky blue depths it lost
the sun's heat. 'Come on.' Francisco was already
swimming, his powerful body cutting through the
turquoise waves with seemingly effortless speed.

'You won't feel the cold once you start swimming.'

And he was right. For the next hour she forgot all the shadows and inconsistencies that had marred the last three weeks as she swam, floated and later paddled at the water's edge while she waited for Francisco, climbing up to the rim of a sand-dune after a while and sitting watching him as he swam with almost Olympic speed and persistence.

He must be exhausted, she thought sleepily as she lay back in the caressing warmth of the sun, shading her eyes against its brilliance. He swam the way he did everything else—with ruthless disregard for any weakness or human frailty and an almost savage determination to drive himself to the limit. What drove him like that? What dark force had him in its grip? Most people found swimming therapeutic. Her thoughts rambled on as the white light beat against her closed eyelids. But she doubted if he did. He wouldn't allow it for a start.

'You will burn the English skin, *infanta*.'

'What?' She started nervously as a dark shadow shut out the sun and then he had dropped down beside her on the warm sand, his body wet and gleaming from the sea.

'The salt water will catch the sun's rays more effectively, you should know this.' His voice was faintly disapproving. 'I do not wish that you should turn lobster-red.'

'I'm not mad about the idea either,' she said flippantly as she tried to control her heartbeat that had gone into racing gear. 'But I'm already quite brown compared to what I was although as most of my sunbathing has been done in this bathing costume I can't really show you the before and after.'

'No, this would not be a good idea.' It was said teasingly but the sudden bolt of lightning in her stomach took her breath away. There was a deepness in the rich voice, a dark heat in the glittering black eyes as they roved over her pale skin that caused flickers of sensation wherever they touched. He wanted her. Physically, at least, he wanted her, she thought painfully, so why couldn't he unbend a little? Why couldn't they communicate? Was there someone else? Was that the reason? Her eyes widened infinitesimally at the thought even as that little inner voice screamed in her head, No! Please, *please* let it be no.

'You've been very kind over the last three weeks, Francisco.' Lorne sat up quickly, hugging her knees to her as she faced him. 'I must have put you to a lot of trouble.'

'Must you?' He lolled back on one elbow lazily as he watched her, his face expressionless.

'Well, with your work schedule and social commitments...' She lowered her head so that a curtain of damp, sea-washed blonde hair swung between them. 'You're obviously a very busy man.'

'I am normally in the fortunate position of holding the reins so it has not proved too exacting a time.' The dark voice was slightly amused. 'Rest assured you have not endangered any million-pound deals or anything else that fertile little mind has been worrying over.'

'Good.' Was he doing it on purpose, she thought tightly, skirting the issue of his private life so adroitly? 'But I wouldn't like any of your...friends to get the wrong impression about me staying at your house.' She didn't dare look up now. 'I'd hate to cause you any embarrassment.'

'My...friends...' he allowed exactly the same tiny pause she had before the word '...would not dare presume in such a way.' It was a definite warning for her to mind her own business.

'Oh.' Set and match to him, she thought angrily. Had he known what she had been asking? Probably. She glanced up now to find the cool, analytical eyes narrowed on her face. 'That's all right, then.'

'Indeed it is.' There was an imperturbability in his voice which she felt sure was intentional. 'I answer to no one but myself, Lorne. I would not have it otherwise.'

'You're very lucky, then, aren't you?' she said quickly. 'Although actually——' She stopped abruptly, aware that what she had been about to say was tactless in the extreme.

'Yes?' he eyed her unsmilingly.

'Oh, nothing.' She shrugged casually.

'Lorne, whenever you open your mouth the one thing that does not come out is nothing,' he said drily. 'You were going to make a comment. Please do so.'

'I was just going to say that it must get lonely at times, being answerable to no one, I mean,' she said weakly. 'I don't think I would describe it as being lucky after all.'

'Then we must agree to differ.' She had annoyed him; she could tell from the stiffening of that square jaw and the hardening of the ebony eyes watching her so tightly. 'I live my life exactly the way I want to. If you choose to interpret it as lonely that is your prerogative but I do not *need* anyone, Lorne. Do you understand me?'

'If you say so.' She ignored the caustic tone and idly traced a pattern in the white sand as though the conversation were perfectly ordinary. 'But you must want a family eventually? A wife, children?'

There was total silence for a few seconds; even the tiny white-crested waves hardly appeared to splash as they ventured up the beach and she didn't dare look at him.

'Must I?' he said at last, his voice sardonic. 'Why?' She did look up then to find the black eyes full of a cold, cynical darkness that was biting. 'To procreate? But perhaps I have no wish to see myself reflected in other human beings. For sex? Neither of us is so naïve to consider marriage necessary for that. For company? Children are tiresome and wives more so.' He was being deliberately hostile and antagonistic and yet there was something, some inflexion in the drawling silky voice, that she didn't understand, that didn't ring true. He appeared to believe what he was saying, his lifestyle bore out the ruthlessly protected bachelor state, and yet . . .

'You still persist in this belief that I am a kind, good man just because I happened to be in the right place at the right time when those youths were having their questionable sport?' He eyed her coldly. 'You do not know me at all, little *infanta*; if you did you would put as much distance between us as you could.'

'You think so,' she said flatly as his cool voice churned up a whole flood of turmoil and confusion. 'Well, if that's the case, why didn't you pack me off the next morning or at least once my ankle was a bit better? I don't understand——'

'That makes two of us.' He had moved over her before she had time to react and when his large shape shut out the sun an immediate and curious weakness took hold of her limbs as his mouth fastened on hers. The tiny pieces of cloth between them seemed woefully inadequate as she felt the leashed power of his big male body, and the flicker of sensual fear that was ever-present in his company sent its tiny shivers of shock shooting down her spine as he penetrated the softness of her mouth. His lips were first coaxingly seductive, then deliberately fierce and erotic as he played havoc with the sensitised flesh of her inner mouth and although she tried to keep a hold on what was happening she felt herself beginning to spin into an ever-increasing vortex of unbearable delight.

An electrifying awareness told her he was good, far too good at this, he must have had hundreds of women... But it didn't matter. All that mattered was his mouth and hands on her face and body and the meltingly violent emotions his expertise were producing on every part of her anatomy.

She couldn't believe her hands had crept up to lock round his hard neck until she felt the crisp dampness of his hair against her fingers, and then, as his mouth trailed a blaze of fire down her throat, neck and into the soft hollow of her breasts, she felt a pleasure that became a torrential warmth.

She should stop this. The inner voice was a shout now. He had just told her in as many words that emotional commitment had no place in his life and here she was allowing... As he peeled the swimming-costume off her breasts so that their full softness was exposed to his gaze she shut her eyes tightly against the harsh passion written in every dark line of his face and then, as his head lowered again to take possession of what his eyes had devoured, she jerked away abruptly, rolling over in the sand on to her stomach as she curled into a tight little ball before pulling the costume back into place and sitting up with a little moan of confusion. 'I'm sorry...' Her hands were clenched fists either side of her burning face. 'I shouldn't have let you do that. I didn't mean to lead you on... I just didn't know——' She stopped abruptly. She was making a painfully embarrassing situation ten times worse. She took a long deep breath to calm her pounding heart and opened her mouth to try again but in the same instant Francisco sat up and placed a finger on her half-open lips.

'This is not a time to talk, *infanta*, and it is I who should apologise.'

She summoned up all her courage and looked into his face, expecting veiled mockery, hidden anger, maybe even contempt or disdain, but the calm, expressionless mask that looked back at her was somehow worse than all these things would have been. How could he, *how could he* make love to her like that and then withdraw so completely into his tough, obdurate shell? Didn't he know how he had affected her? She would never have believed a man's touch could hold such dangerous power; she had been mindless beneath his caresses, and to dismiss her like this so... so casually... She didn't know a thing about him, not a thing beyond that he frightened her half to death with his effortless mastery over her reason, the very quintessence of her mind.

He had the power to break her. The thought flashed into her consciousness as she stared at his handsome, proud face. He could break her, carelessly and without even knowing, and she didn't understand why. She hadn't known he existed a month ago and now——

'Let us return for lunch.'

'Lunch?' She felt as though she had just been pulled backwards through an emotional mangle and the man was talking about lunch? The spurt of anger was red-hot and with it came face-saving dignity. He wanted to push the whole episode, and her, away? Slot it into one of the ice-cool compartments in that arctic mind labelled 'finished'? Well, two can play at that game, she thought savagely. 'Lunch? Lovely,' she said brightly. 'I'm absolutely starving.' I hate you, I hate you, her mind was screaming at him as they walked back up the beach, and she was amazed he couldn't hear. She knew she was being illogical, that she should be relieved he had taken the rebuff with such good grace, but instead the urge to hit him was growing with every silent step. And if events had escalated to their natural conclusion? If she hadn't stopped him? She kept her face straight ahead as she marched rigidly up the beach. He would probably have rolled over with much the same lack of warmth when he had finished. A need would have been satisfied, a hunger fed, but it wouldn't have touched his heart at all. If he had one. Which she doubted!

Rosa had prepared a veritable banquet on their return, a beautifully set little table complete with crystal wine glasses and silver cutlery laid out in majestic splendour on the sun-soaked veranda with a small bowl of sweet-smelling freesias in centre place, their delicate white and yellow petals giving off a rich perfume that scented the air with summer.

'Oh, Rosa, this is lovely but you shouldn't have gone to so much trouble,' Lorne said impulsively, her eyes widening at the proof of such careful thought and attention to detail on the part of the little Spanish woman. 'A sandwich would have been fine.'

'A sandwich?' From Rosa's scandalised expression Lorne assumed, correctly, that she had committed sacrilege.

'I think Lorne is quite overwhelmed,' Francisco put in smoothly behind her, 'as I am.'

Rosa beamed immediately and gestured to the door leading into the hall. 'You wish to shower, *señorita*? I show you the bathroom, *sí*? And then you enjoy the lunch much better.'

Lorne followed the small figure into the hall and up one flight of stairs to the large bathroom, touched to see that her clothes had been brought from the downstairs cloakroom while they had swum and laid out carefully in preparation for her return, along with brushes, combs, shampoo and a wide selection of creams and lotions.

'I very glad to see you, *señorita*.' Rosa had stood aside for Lorne to enter the room but now moved in quickly behind her, shutting the door carefully and standing with her back to it. 'The *señor* has been alone for too long.'

'I'm sorry?' Lorne took a step towards Rosa uncertainly. The little Spanish woman had spoken in such a quiet soft voice that she wasn't sure if she had heard her correctly. 'I'm just staying with him for a few days, that's all.'

'No.' Rosa shook her head determinedly. 'This is not all, not with the *señor*. I see the way he look at you; I wait for this for many years.'

'Rosa——'

'This is *his* place, his *special* place, you understand?' The bright black eyes had fastened on Lorne's soft grey ones with such a fierce intensity that Lorne couldn't break the hold. 'He never bring anyone here, not even in the old days when everything OK. And when it happen he come here to grieve, to get well, but it not OK, it never OK.'

She could only follow half of the small woman's urgent low words but gathered she was speaking about the days following the accident.

'He is good man, *sí*? Very good man, but you must not let him send you away,' Rosa said quickly with a quick darting glance to the door as the sound of her name was heard from downstairs. 'You can help him, I know this, I feel it here.' She touched her flat bosom with the palm of her hand. 'I go now. You say nothin', nothin'.'

She had disappeared before Lorne could gather her wits sufficiently to ask her to stay. What did all that mean? She moved across to the shower cubicle in the corner of the room and regulated the water to a warm flow, her mind dissecting Rosa's words over and over again as she washed her hair and dressed hastily. She must talk with the housekeeper properly; she felt she had the key to the mystery that surrounded Francisco and his whole household. But Rosa had got one thing wrong. She glanced at her reflection in the long mirror at the side of the door as she left the room, seeing only a too-slim wide-eyed young girl in the faintly misty glass and missing the ethereal beauty and pure clean loveliness that looked back

at her. She couldn't help Francisco. He moved
in a world of elegant, sophisticated, wordly-wise
women who were as beautiful as they were in-
telligent. Maybe one of them could reach the
stony heart of this cold, dark Spanish man but
she had neither the knowledge nor experience of
men necessary to penetrate his reserve. Look at
this morning. She shut her eyes tightly and then
took a long deep breath as she opened the door.
She had behaved like a nervous schoolgirl on her
first date, or worse. No. She couldn't help him,
if he needed help, that was.

She didn't have a chance to talk to Rosa again;
indeed it seemed as if Francisco deliberately fore-
stalled any opportunity for her to be alone with
the little housekeeper although that was probably
just her imagination. When she had joined him
at the lunch table he had been cool and enigmatic, his conversation faintly mocking and
cynical and his eyes deliberately cold.

A shadow had fallen over the day and when
they had finished lunch and Francisco suggested
a walk along the beach he made no effort to take
her hand or touch her in any way, his whole attitude suggesting he was regretting asking her to
come.

'Francisco?' They had walked for some considerable distance in silence and as they reached
another tiny cove which the murmuring sea was
invading with determined purpose, flooding over
smooth mounds of polished rock to run quickly
up the thick sand, she felt a sudden hot rebellion
as she followed at his heels.

'Yes?' He turned immediately, his black eyes hooded and remote and his hands pushed deep in his trouser pockets.

'Can we sit a while?' She indicated the vast sweep of sea and sky with a wave of her hand. 'All this exercise is a little hard to take in one go.'

'I'm sorry, Lorne.' He smiled but it didn't reach the guarded eyes. 'I should have known better. Is your ankle hurting?'

'A little.' She noted with a dart of helpless anger that he seated himself at least three feet away. What did he think she was going to do, for goodness' sake? Fling herself on him? 'But it's OK.'

'Good.' His voice was as distant as his body and the urge to do something outrageous to get his attention properly tingled temptingly along her veins. She hadn't felt the sensation since she was a child when she had often considered that Tom got more than his fair share of fuss from her mother, and she cautioned herself quickly. She was a fully grown adult now even if *he* didn't seem to think so at times.

'The villa is very lovely,' she said quietly after several long minutes of silence as she glanced at his grim profile. 'Did you come here for holidays when you were a boy?'

He stiffened slightly at the reference to his childhood but his voice was quiet and impersonal as he spoke. 'Yes. For most of the summer, very often. My father was always a very busy man and liked to entertain often so my mother usually stayed with him. Rosa and Josef would look after us; they are more like family than anything else.' The 'us' must mean his brother, sister and himself, she thought quickly. 'We had some fun.' The dark eyes moved over to meet hers slowly. 'Midnight barbecues and so on. The usual things children and teenagers do.'

She nodded, her voice encouraging. 'Yes?'

'And your childhood? Did you have holidays by the sea?'

That was it? she thought with a swift shaft of disappointment. No more revelations, if the few words he had uttered could be called that.

'A few.' She kept her voice casual and friendly as though she were unaware of the overt antagonism that was keeping his body taut and tight. 'Once Mum and Dad died that was it, though, of course; there was no money for luxuries like holidays any more.'

'No, of course not.' He nodded as he turned to look straight ahead again.

The silence stretched on interminably this time and, although she had vowed to herself that she wouldn't be the one to break it, after ten minutes her nerves were stretched to breaking-point. 'Is anything wrong, Francisco?' Her voice sounded over-loud in the empty air, the slow swishing of the sea barely registering on her senses. 'Is it what happened before lunch?' Crass, crass, crass, Lorne, she muttered silently in her head as soon as the words were out.

'Before lunch?' He turned to look at her again as though he had no idea of what she was talking about.

'I did apologise.' Her voice was painfully taut now. 'I didn't mean to lead you on——'

'Don't, Lorne.' There was a harshness in the quiet words that hurt her. 'What do you want me to say? That I understand, that it was all my fault? Well, I *can* say that and mean it. If you want me to pretend I do not want you as well that is beyond me. This is not easy and I am trying to do the right thing——'

'Don't you ever let yourself go?' she interrupted him deliberately. 'I mean, *ever*? It's not a crime to want to kiss me, is it?'

'But I do not want just to *kiss* you, Lorne,' he said with slow and unmistakable emphasis, 'and you know that full well. I am not a promiscuous man but neither am I a saint. The women I mix with——' He stopped abruptly.

'Yes?' She stood up now, walking down to the water's edge, which was bathed in fiery colour as the sun began to sink slowly into the sea and keeping her back towards him as she gazed out over the rippling waves.

'They are quite different from you,' he said flatly behind her.

Different? What does that mean? she thought painfully. More beautiful, interesting, certainly more experienced! Why did this hurt so much? Why couldn't she be as cool as he?

She knew if she spoke the pain that had her chest in an iron band would reflect in her voice so she nodded jerkily in silence, the fresh, salty air warm and tangy against her face. He must have thought she was such a fool when she had pushed him away earlier. The thought had the power to put scarlet in her cheeks. No doubt his usual women would have handled the situation smoothly and with great femininity, with it resulting in satisfied pleasure for both parties. Instead she had reacted like a scalded cat. Her head drooped a little and she forced the hot tears that were hovering at the back of her eyes from falling with tremendous will-power.

'Rosa and Josef like you.' He had moved to stand just behind her and she concentrated hard on the pink-slashed water. 'She normally takes her time before dishing out approval but you seem to have been an instant hit.'

'I liked her too.' She tried to make her voice light and casual, she really did try, but even to her own ears the thick husky note spoke of suppressed tears.

'Oh, *infanta*...' He moved closer to her, his arms slipping round her waist as he pulled her backwards into his hard, firm body, his chin resting on the top of her head as he nuzzled the warm silkiness of her hair. 'You smell like all my summers rolled into one, so good...' She tensed at first, longing to turn round in his arms and seek his mouth but knowing the timing was all wrong, and gradually, as they stood as one with the vast glittering expanse of the ocean into which the sky was pouring flaming rivers of scarlet, gold and orange, she began to relax. Curiously the

motionless embrace was more intimate than anything that had gone before and more agonisingly
sweet.

When he took her hand and led her back along
the beach they still didn't speak, and once at the
villa he refused Rosa's offer of dinner, leaving
within minutes for the long drive home. 'You do
not mind?' His eyes were dark and distant on
Lorne's face. 'There is work in my study which
I must look at tonight.'

'Of course not.' She knew he was lying, that
the unspoken intimacy had bothered him more
than he cared to admit, and as they drove through
the dusk-filled evening she realised she had never
been so confused and bewildered in her life.

They arrived back at the house as the last of
the daylight fled and as the car glided to a smooth
halt under the enormous cedar tree she forced
herself to look quietly into his face. 'Thank you
for a lovely day; I enjoyed it.'

'Liar.' He echoed the accusation her mind had
thrown at her even as she spoke. 'It was a
mockery of a day and you know it.' For a second
he looked painfully, overwhelmingly weary, the
lines round his mouth and eyes more deeply
etched in the shadowed darkness and his eyes as
black as coal. 'I have made you very unhappy,
haven't I?' It was a statement that did not re-
quire an answer. 'I should have followed my first
instinct and sent you home the next day after I
found you.' There was a frightening inflexibility
in the low voice. 'Instead . . .' He shook his head

slowly. 'I am a selfish man, *infanta*, a ruthless, selfish man.'

'I don't think you are.' Suddenly all the agony and humiliation of the day was washed away in the face of his pain. 'You've been good to me.' And as she said it it seemed true. All she wanted to do was to comfort him, to be there for him, to be near him. She couldn't bear not to be near him.

'Good to you?' he said incredulously, his face full of an anguish she didn't understand. 'The hell I have. Go home, Lorne. Go home now before it's too late.'

'You're sending me away?' Her voice was small and her eyes huge as she stared up into his dark face.

'I wish I had the strength to do that.' Now there was a savage anger in his voice that made her shrink back against the beautifully upholstered seat. 'But you are beautiful and desirable and I want you. I want to possess your body, Lorne, to be the first, you know this?' He was being cruel and they both knew it. 'And then I would let you go, *make* you go if necessary.' His eyes were icy with self-hatred as they held hers. 'And you can still say I have been good to you?'

'Don't talk like that.' She found the strength from somewhere to answer him. 'It isn't really you, so don't do it.'

'What do you know of me?' He gave a harsh laugh that jarred her senses. 'What do you really know of me? You might be attracted to the outward man, to that which you can see with the

naked eye. But so have many others.' His gaze
was unrelenting on her white face. 'I have had
many women who have enjoyed the pleasures of
love in my arms; you would be nothing new. This
is the man you cannot see.'

'Stop it, Francisco.' She drew herself up
straight although she was shaking so much he
couldn't fail to see it. 'I won't listen to this.
You're trying to make me hate you and you can't,
you can't.' She wrenched open the door on a little
sob of pain and stumbled from the car in the
darkness. He made no attempt to follow her,
sitting like a great frozen statue in the magnificent car as she ran towards the house, her long
blonde hair catching the slivers of moonlight that
flickered down beneath the trees.

As she brushed past Alfonso in the hall she
was vaguely aware of his astonished eyes on her
face but she didn't stop until she had reached the
sanctuary of her room, falling on to the bed after
locking the door in an agony of weeping that
continued for long soul-searching minutes. She
didn't hate him, she could never hate him, but
how she did feel she didn't know. She shook her
head as the tears subsided to gentle hiccups. No,
that wasn't quite true, she dared not know. She
dared not probe that part of her that he had taken
for his own, not if she wanted to remain whole.

But one thing she *did* know. She sat up suddenly in the blackness as she rubbed a hand over
her wet face. He was not the cruel monster he
would have her believe. She wasn't aware of how
she had arrived at her knowledge, it was

compounded of so many things, so many facets of his complicated personality that she had seen over the last three weeks, but deep inside she was absolutely sure. And she would not be shaken from her belief. Not by him, not by anyone. It was as well she didn't know, as she sat in the quiet room full of the scent of the summer's night, how severely that decision would be tested in the days ahead.

# CHAPTER SEVEN

THE next few days ticked by with interminable slowness. Francisco left the house each morning immediately after breakfast, returning just before dinner, which was eaten in the large dining-room in formal silence and splendour. The first evening Lorne tried to make conversation but when her efforts were met with an unconcealed contempt she withdrew into a proud silence that she maintained each night. Two can play at this game, Francisco de Vega, she thought balefully each evening as she forced food past the huge lump in her throat. I can keep this up just as long as you can. She took comfort from the fact that no plane tickets arrived on her dressing-table although she steeled herself each day in case it happened. And if it did she would go, she had made up her mind about that. But she couldn't be the one to suggest it. She would regret it for the rest of her life if she did, the not knowing, the not being sure of something she couldn't even put into thoughts, let alone words. He had to *make* her leave.

'You're a real confused mess,' she said drily to the wan-faced reflection in the mirror as she dressed on the morning of the fifth day after the disastrous visit to the beach-house. 'No wonder he thinks you aren't safe to be let out alone.'

As soon as she entered the breakfast-room that morning she sensed something was different, that he had made some sort of a decision. 'Good morning, Lorne.' The smile was formal but he actually looked at her this morning instead of at a point somewhere over her left shoulder. 'I have just discovered my presence is required in Geneva next week so I think we will have to regard the next few days as our last together.' The smile faltered for a moment at the naked hurt in her face and then was forced back rigidly into place. 'Is there anywhere in particular you would like to see?'

'What?' She forgot to act, forgot to play the cool woman of the world in the face of his cold dismissal.

'I thought we could do a little sightseeing?' The tone was pleasant and relaxed and she was too upset to see the tightly clenched jaw and white knuckles as he gripped the edge of the table. 'Before you go home to England?'

'Oh, please don't bother,' she said tightly as a surge of colour flooded into her white face. 'I'm sure you must be very busy and I would hate to disrupt such a hectic schedule.' She poured herself a cup of strong coffee as she spoke and wondered for the briefest of moments where she had left her stomach.

'Now you are being childish,' he said calmly. 'You have always been aware that I have business interests to oversee; I cannot play the holiday-maker forever.'

'Is that what you've been doing?' She eyed him furiously. 'I'd never have guessed,' she added with deep sarcasm.

'I can see you are incapable of deciding for yourself so I will make the decision for you,' he said smoothly. 'The fortress of Guadalest is not too far away and I understand there is a fiesta in a nearby town tonight. We will go there. It will be both educational and amusing.'

She glared at him without answering as he stood slowly, magnificent and darkly handsome in loose-fitting grey cotton trousers and a white cotton shirt that sat on his big body with comfortable ease. 'Enjoy your breakfast and I will assume you will be ready in an hour,' he said evenly as he walked lazily from the room.

For a crazy moment she almost obeyed the impulse to throw the coffee-cup after him but restrained herself just in time. What was she getting upset for, after all? He hadn't promised a thing, he certainly didn't owe her anything; just the opposite, in fact. It was he who had rescued her, provided her with board and lodging, stepped into the breach when she was hurt and helpless. But that didn't make it any easier to take. She ground her teeth together in an agony of impotent rage. So she had been wrong. It was as simple as that. All these half-formed ideas and feelings were rubbish. He had offered her shelter for a time and now he wanted to get rid of her. End of story. As he said, he was cold and ruthless and hard and the confines of living in close proximity with such a man for the last few weeks had caused a temporary imbalance of mind. She would look at it like that. *She would*. And what she felt for him? Physical attraction, animal desire. She wouldn't dress it up as anything else. She would probably meet loads of men who would affect her in the same way in her lifetime. The ridiculousness of the thought mocked her as she forced the slices of grapefruit, grilled in rum and brown sugar, that Teresa had just placed in front of her past the obstruction in her throat. Absolutely loads.

She was sitting waiting in prim silence for him just under an hour later when he appeared from his study, her hair in a neat shiny ponytail, her face devoid of a trace of make-up and her eyes downcast on the hands folded in her lap.

'Very submissive.' One black eyebrow slanted in sardonic amusement. 'I wonder how long you can keep it up?'

'I don't know what you mean,' she said icily as she raised her grey gaze to his.

'The little-whipped-dog approach——'

She cut the drawling voice short with an angry exclamation. 'How dare you? I'm no more like a whipped dog——' She stopped abruptly as she saw dark humour in the wicked black eyes.

'Exactly...' he checked the gold watch on his wrist with slow enjoyment '...ten seconds. That must be a record even for you.' As she went to reply he covered the few feet between them in two strides, pulling her to her feet and placing a finger on her mouth as her lips opened. 'We've only a few days left and I would like to enjoy the

time we have together. Can we forget all that has
gone before and just...be? No questions, no
tomorrows? *Sí*?'

She stared at him in surprise, annoyance
warring with bewilderment. What was the cause
of this mercurial change-about? The fact that she
would be gone in a few days and he could get on
with his life again? And yet if that were the case
he could have packed her off any time in the last
three weeks. And it had been his suggestion that
he spend time with her, show her a taste of local
colour. She didn't understand him. She didn't
understand him at all.

'Well?' He was impossibly handsome and
darkly masculine as he stood there surveying her
with slightly narrowed eyes, the subtle, delicious
smell of him undermining her resolve to remain
cool and distant and totally unapproachable. 'Do
we take what fate has given us even if the sand
in the hour-glass is nearly gone? I will not force
you to come with me, *infanta*. I do not have the
right.'

'You talk as though nothing is changeable, as
though your fate is already decided,' she said
faintly. 'My father used to say that fifty per cent
of our destiny is chance and the other half is in
our own hands to do with what we will. You don't
have to accept the cards you've been given if you
don't like them, don't you see——?'

'What I see is a very beautiful and courageous
young woman who deserves the best out of life.'
She had never noticed before how the deep
grooves in his cheeks slashed the taut brown skin

but suddenly he looked desperately tired, tired and painfully sad. She stared at him in stricken silence. She knew instinctively that she had been given her answer and it was no good to continue the conversation.

'I'd like to come with you, Francisco,' she said slowly, 'very much.'

'Good.' He smiled softly. 'Then let us go.'

Lorne was to remember that day for the rest of her life as a bittersweet enchanted time in which the minutes ticked by far too quickly, and each glance from Francisco, each touch of his hand was unbearably, poignantly precious.

The solid fortress of Guadalest, perched on its high rocky pinnacle and inaccessible except via a tunnel through fifty feet of rock, was majestically ancient, making the sleepy villages they drove through later, with their mazes of cobbled streets, simple granite churches and tiny walled gardens adjoining rich orchards, seem all the lighter and more colourful by comparison.

They passed tiny little white cottages nestling alone at the edge of rough roads against a wonderful backdrop of craggy mountains and pine-clad hills, where hens, chickens and small dark pigs lived on terms of comradeship with their owners, wandering happily in and out of ever-open doors, and when they eventually stopped for a late lunch at a wayside tavern she found to her surprise that she was hungry for the first time in days.

'Try the ham,' Francisco whispered in her ear as the landlady rattled through the menu in rapid

Spanish. 'The Extremaduran sierra is the only place in the country that supports the pure-bred Iberian pig and it is the source of the best *jamón serrano*. I promise you will love it.'

'I will?' She wouldn't care what she ate, Lorne thought dreamily as she stared into his dark face. This is what it could be like. The thought had been hammering in her brain all day. The two of them together, laughing, talking, being content with just each other. It was as though he had given her a glimpse of heaven, which made the thought of her departure in the next few days all the more mystifying.

'For the ham to be as highly flavoured as possible the pig is allowed to run wild and eat acorns for several months of the year,' Francisco continued softly. 'The taste is...unimaginable.'

'It sounds perfect.'

And it was. Like the rest of the day. In the soft pink dusk of late evening they arrived at the fiesta in time to see a gay procession of darkly dashing riders on horseback performing amazing feats of acrobatics and juggling while controlling their high-spirited mounts. The firework display started as soon as night fell along with a brightly lit fair that brought dark flashing girls in bright summer dresses, smiling coquettishly at the groups of youths eyeing them under black slanting brows.

She couldn't believe this was the same grim-faced, coldly austere man who had made the last few days so miserable when Francisco wrapped her tightly in his arms as the whirling machines whisked them laughing into the air, the smell and feel of him encompassing every part of her as she wished the evening would never end. But it did. As she had known it would.

As they left the fairground he drew her gently into his arms just before they reached the patiently waiting Ferrari which crouched quietly in the shadows, tracing the outline of her mouth with a tender finger as he looked into her face as though trying to memorise every feature, every eyelash. And the kiss, when it came, was hot and potent, a raging need taking control of her as he devoured her mouth, desire a raging fire in him that was spreading with dangerous intensity. He was muttering her name as though it was a talisman against fate, drawing her into him so that his powerful body loomed over her and she could feel every muscle, every male contour of his hard shape as intimately as though they were naked.

When he moved her away reluctantly she saw a rueful smile touch the firm mouth. 'Now you see why I did not kiss you in the car,' he said thickly. 'I cannot trust myself where you are concerned, *pequeña.*'

'Perhaps I don't want you to,' she said weakly as the taste of him still spun in her head.

'Ah, you say this now because the night is dark and scented with flowers and there is romance in the air,' he said quietly. 'In the morning, in the many mornings that would follow when you were all alone and I was gone, you would regret such foolishness. I will not take your innocence from you, Lorne. When you give it it must be to someone who is free to love you in return.'

'There's someone else?' She stared at him with huge haunted eyes. 'Another woman?'

'No.' He had hesitated for a long moment before he replied but she knew he was telling the truth. 'It would be easier if there were, but no, I will not lie to you. There is no one else. But nevertheless any emotional attachment between us is not possible.'

'But why——?'

He stopped her with a light kiss as he turned her round and pushed her towards the car. 'No questions. We agreed.'

She must have slept on the way home because it seemed as though it was only minutes before Francisco was shaking her gently, his eyes soft in the lights from the house. 'We are home, Lorne.'

Home? The simple sentence haunted her for half of the night as she lay restlessly tossing and turning in a half-doze that brought all her fears and heartaches to the fore. It was *his* home; it could never be hers. But she wasn't going to spoil the short time they had left together with any more unwelcome probing enquiries. She would just... be. As he had said.

That resolution was in the front of her mind later the next afternoon when the cataclysm reached out to devour her. They had spent the morning alternately swimming and sunbathing in a little hideaway cove overlooking the scintillatingly clear blue sea before getting dressed and driving into the country again in the afternoon

to eat the picnic they had brought with them at
her suggestion. Francisco had been both surprised and delighted at the idea, and as they finished the last of the food spread out on the huge
car rug in a little grassy dell they had found he
smiled at her slowly, his dark brown eyes soft
and velvet-like.

'I have not indulged myself like this since I was
a youth,' he said quietly. 'I had forgotten how
good a simple meal can be in the open air. My
brother and I used to walk miles with rucksacks
on our backs that never seemed to grow heavy.
We were sometimes gone for days at a time, but
our parents never worried. They felt Carlos was
safe with me.'

'I'm sure he was.' She tried to keep all emotion
out of her voice. This was the first time he had
spoken about his brother and she felt any un-
toward interest from herself and he would shut
up like a clam. 'My parents felt exactly the same
when I was with Tom.'

'And they never had cause to regret their trust.'
His voice was bleak and she hardly dared breathe
as she glanced at his face rent with violent harsh
emotion. 'As mine would have if they had lived.'

'I don't understand.' She had to say something. The pain in his face was causing an ache
in her throat that was unbearable. 'Your brother
died in an accident; it can't have been your fault.'

'An accident?' The change in him was
lightning-fast and all the more shocking for its
swiftness. The old Francisco was back, cold, hard

and fierce as he glared into her face. 'What do you know of this?'

'Someone just mentioned——'

'Someone?' He almost snarled the word, his face black. 'And this someone has a name?'

'A name?' She stared at him, stunned by the ferocity of the attack. 'It doesn't matter——'

'It matters.' He had been sprawling on one elbow on the springy grass but now in one swift movement he was upright, bending over and pulling her to her feet in the next breath. 'Who told you?'

She couldn't betray Alfonso. Her thoughts raced as his hand dug painfully into her arm. The old servant had clearly known Francisco would react like this when she had had to drag the information from him. She couldn't give the old man away. 'I can't say.' She raised her chin a fraction. 'I'm sorry.'

'The hell you are.' He let go of her arm abruptly and moved back a pace, his eyes vitriolic. 'You have been poking and prying into things that do not concern you, you understand me?'

'Understand you?' The last thread of her control slipped as she realised they were back days ago, all the precious time in between counting for nothing in the blackness of his rage. He was inhuman. 'Understand you!' Her voice was a shriek now but she didn't care, standing in front of him like a tiny trapped animal that had suddenly found the courage to turn on its hunter. 'No, I don't understand you. I doubt if anyone could. You talk in nothing but riddles and I've never known anyone who is so many different people. How could I possibly *understand* you? You're not normal!'

'I will not argue with you, Lorne,' he said with arrogant coldness. 'You will tell me who spoke to you of my private affairs. *Now*!'

'No, I won't.' Suddenly she hated him, fiercely and bitterly, for hurting her like this. 'You don't own me; you can't order me about the way you do everyone else. I won't have it.'

'I see.' The acid contempt in his eyes was like a sharp slap on the face. 'You are a free spirit, doing "your own thing", is that it?'

'Don't twist my words again.' The flare of colour in her cheeks was in marked contrast to her white face.

'Again?' The black eyebrows rose in haughty enquiry. 'I was not aware I had done so before.'

'You might not be "aware" of it,' she said bitterly, 'but you do it all the time. It's one of your little protective devices, isn't it, to stop anyone getting too close, to keep them at the required distance?'

'Now you are being ridiculous.' She had hit him on the raw. She saw it in the way the near-ebony eyes narrowed into black slits, his mouth a harsh slash in the taut face. 'And we are not discussing me. I want to know exactly what you were told.'

'I wasn't told anything that I should imagine isn't common knowledge,' she said angrily. 'There was an accident some years ago on the family yacht. Your mother and brother and his

family and some servants were killed. That's all.
What's so wrong in my knowing that?'

'And that is all that was said, those bare facts?'
His eyes were diamond-hard on her face. 'I shall
know if you lie to me.'

'For goodness' sake...' She raised her hands
helplessly as she shook her head in bewilderment. 'There isn't more, is there?'

'No.' He held her confused eyes for a long tense
minute before turning away abruptly, every line
of his big body expressing furious rage and tight
control. 'There is nothing more. Get in the car.'

'What?'

'I said get in the car.' He began to throw the
picnic things into the back of the Ferrari with
furious precision.

'I'd rather crawl than get in there with you.'
For a minute she thought he hadn't heard her
low, shaking voice but he froze for a endless
moment before swinging round to face her, and
she saw murderous rage in the glittering eyes.

'Do not push me any further, Lorne,' he said
tersely.

'I mean it.' She took a step backwards in spite
of herself, intimidated by his sheer strength and
power. 'I don't want anything more to do with
you.'

'I can assure you the feeling is mutual,' he said
icily as his face twisted as though in pain, 'but
as you are miles from anywhere with no means
of transportation you will have to endure my
company for a short time longer.'

'What's the matter with you?' she asked faintly as the enormity of the confrontation washed over her, leaving her trembling and sick. 'You were so different yesterday. How can you be like this now?'

'So different?' He took a shuddering breath, his eyes bleak. 'Maybe I was in danger of forgetting...'

'Forgetting?' She couldn't bear the pain in his face and suddenly flew to his side, grasping his arms as she looked up into the dark face above her. 'Tell me, Francisco, what is it?'

As he stared down at her something worked in his face that was terrifyingly harrowing and just for a moment, as she felt the deep searing pain that was strangling the words in his throat, she thought he was going to confide in her, to open the door that would let her in. But then that deadly control took over again and his face became a remote mask that she couldn't see through.

'You have to understand the way things are here,' he said in a cold, tight voice as he carefully extricated himself from her hold and moved to sit on the bonnet of the car, his black hair gleaming in the white sunlight and his long legs powerful under their covering of light cotton. 'For a man such as I duty comes first.' She stared at him blindly, feeling very small and very alone as the deep voice churned relentlessly on. 'When I marry it will be to secure an heir whose mother will be from a family of equal influence and standing as befits the name of Vega. I may...indulge certain needs in the meantime but I will not allow myself to be distracted from responsibilities I have as sole heir. The family name, my business interests, are of vital importance to the sons that will follow me one day. I will never permit anything to get in the way of that, anything at all.'

She kept her eyes fixed on the darkness of his as she struggled to take in what he had said, and then as a flood of burning anger replaced the shock and hurt she drew herself up to her full five feet four, her soft grey eyes taking the texture of burnished steel. 'I don't understand why you are telling me this,' she said with an icy control that matched his. 'It is of no interest to me whom or why you marry; we are virtual strangers, after all.' She wanted to hurt him, wanted to see some reaction in that cool aristocratic face that was watching her so carefully, but the control held and she could see nothing in the expressionless features in front of her. 'I need to sort things out with Sancho before I leave Spain so it's probably better if I leave tomorrow anyway, if that's convenient?'

'Sancho?' He moved so swiftly off the car and to her side that he was a blur. 'You will have nothing to do with that boy, do you hear me? He is no good for you.'

She had absolutely no intention of trying to see Sancho ever again but she wasn't going to tell him that. She had pulled his name out of the hat to save the pride which Francisco had just trampled into the dust, and in view of the way

Sancho had treated her she figured he owed her
something, albeit a posthumous reckoning. 'I
thought I'd made it clear that you can't tell me
what to do,' she said tightly, her face as white as
a sheet. 'You have no right——'

'Damn my right!' He took hold of her arms
roughly, shaking her like a dog with a bone. 'He
is worthless, do you not see this? He will not take
care of you——'

'I don't want anyone to take care of me.' She
raised her chin proudly. 'I can take care of myself;
I've been doing it for years.'

He swore, softly but with great intensity in his
native tongue, before pulling her against him so
violently that her breath caught in her throat at
the impact. She began to struggle wildly but he
held her so firmly that she had to stop after a
time, recognising that her protests were as inef-
fectual as a little moth caught up in a thunder-
storm. And then he kissed her, lifting her face to
his with one hand as he took her lips in a searing
kiss that seemed to brand her very soul. 'I will
not allow you to see this man again . . .' he was
muttering feverishly against her skin as he
covered her face and throat in blazing kisses that
she was powerless to resist, and even though she
was still lucid enough to see the injustice, the
unfairness of his words she couldn't do anything
about it. Her whole being was caught up in the
feel and closeness of him and she was lost, totally,
helplessly lost.

She wasn't sure if he pulled her to the ground
or she fell there, but as she felt the thick springy

grass beneath her back and the weight of him above she opened her eyes wide for one second before he took her mouth again. His hands were sensuous and warm as they wandered over her body, his touch creating a need that was devastating. She knew he didn't love her, knew he wasn't prepared to make any commitment for the future, and yet in spite of that she didn't have the will to push him away. Her emotions had been on a see-saw ever since she met him and yet she couldn't imagine a world without him. It was crazy, totally insane, but she wanted him in a way she had never imagined it was possible to feel.

'You are so beautiful, so fresh...' It was the last word that stirred something in her mind, pulled her back from the edge of total capitulation. He had told her, *told her* that he wanted her because she was a virgin, that he wanted to be the first. And he had told her that he would leave her afterwards. In cold blood. Without emotion. *What was she doing?*

He made no effort to stop her as she pushed against him and sat up, stumbling to her feet and walking across to the car with trembling legs. 'I want to go back, Francisco.' She knew her voice was flat and dead-sounding but her pride, her self-esteem was all gone. She was a novelty, nothing more, and it was time she faced it.

'Lorne, you must understand——'

'I will never understand you.' As she swung round to take in his face, ashen and heavy-eyed, she almost weakened, but it had to be said, calmly and coolly. 'I don't *understand* what is so special about a family name, I don't *understand* how you can judge one person against another on account of their background or wealth, I don't *understand* how you can be so cold about everything. I just wouldn't accept it, would I...?' Her eyes were grey pools of pain. 'I wanted to believe...' She shook her head slowly. 'And you told me. I have to admit you told me.' He stared at her unmoving as inside she slowly shrivelled up. 'It's life and love that really count, Francisco, two people creating a family out of their shared love regardless of whether they are paupers or princes, rich or poor. Children don't care if their father is a dustman or a king as long as they're loved and wanted and cared for. And your children will miss out.' She brushed a wisp of hair from her cheek wearily. 'Oh, they might be rich, have everything that money can buy with family connections they can trace back to goodness knows where, but they will have two parents who married for all the wrong reasons and will always remain two parents, never joined as one.'

'Have you finished?' His voice was expressionless.

'Yes, I've finished,' she said tiredly, 'except to say that I pity you, Francisco de Vega, from the bottom of my heart. I pity your empty aspirations, your hollow outlook, your whole shallow existence, and I wish I had never met you.'

'I appreciate your frankness.' His voice was cutting now but somehow it didn't penetrate the numbness that had taken over her mind, her whole body, and which enabled her to face him without shattering into a hundred little pieces. 'If you are *sure* you have finished we will leave.'

'Don't you ever wonder, just for a minute, if maybe you are wrong?' she asked flatly as he gestured towards the car. 'Don't you ever doubt yourself? Wonder if you are missing it?'

'No.' He held her eyes steadily as he spoke. 'I faced all my personal goblins years ago. I know exactly where I am going and how to get there.'

'It doesn't seem to have made you very happy,' she said slowly as a certain inflexion in the deep voice chilled her blood.

'*Happy*?' He held the word on his tongue as though it was repulsive to him. 'I am not looking for happiness.' If anyone else had said it she would have felt they were playing a part, perhaps trying to project an image that was mysterious for some diverse purpose of their own. But he *meant* it. The chill increased in strength. He really meant it.

'Why?' She shook her head slowly. 'Why aren't you?'

'You do not want to know.' The words were as cold as ice. 'Believe me, Lorne, you do not want to know.' He moved to her side and opened the car door with a dismissive gesture that was like a slap in the face and as she slid into the car's warm interior she felt she understood him less now than when she had first met him.

## CHAPTER EIGHT

FRANCISCO didn't speak once on the journey
home and neither did Lorne; her whole being was
concentrated on holding on to the anaesthetising
numbness that had taken her over, hugging the
blank insensibility to her as a blanket against the
coldness of her spirit. Her mind dissected the
harsh words she had spoken with a kind of
remote detachment as though she had been an
observer watching a dramatic play, a tragedy, and
as yet she was too dazed to feel either remorse
or regret.

'I've got a splitting headache. Could you tell
Teresa I'll miss dinner?' She had spoken in the
curiously stunned, trance-like mode her thoughts
were in and after a swift glance at her white face
Francisco nodded curtly, his face cold.

'Of course.'

Once in her room she sat on the bed for what
seemed like hours but was in reality only thirty
minutes or so, her limbs heavy and lethargic and
the headache of which she had spoken a definite
throbbing at the back of her skull. Eventually
she persuaded herself into the shower, standing
under the clear warm water for long minutes with
her eyes shut and her head uplifted. She was
leaving. Her heart thudded painfully and she
clenched her hands together across the softness

of her breasts. She wouldn't think of it now. Later, perhaps.

'*Señorita*?' Teresa's voice outside the bathroom and the sharp knock on the door forced her to wrap a big bath-sheet hastily round her wet body and after looping her hair into a small hand-towel she opened the door carefully.

'Yes?'

'I bring the tray, *señorita*.' Teresa indicated the small table to the left of her. 'The *señor*, he say you feel bad with the headache so he tell me to serve you dinner here. He send the pills for the headache that you have first, *sí*?'

'Thank you, Teresa.' Lorne found a smile from somewhere. She didn't want his kindness; he could take his dinner and——

'I come back later.' Teresa nodded towards the tray heaped with a selection of cold meats, salad and small spicy potatoes, alongside of which was placed a very large wine glass full of light sparkling rosé. 'You eat now.'

After the small maid had skuttled away Lorne glanced helplessly at the vast array of food and then pushed the tray to one side after taking the pills along with a few sips of wine. She couldn't eat, it would choke her. Nothing could get past the painful lump in her throat. She hadn't wanted it to end like this. She closed her eyes as her mind ticked on and forced her to face the truth. She hadn't wanted it to end at all! But if she started to think, to allow her brain to function properly, this pain that was being held at bay would become a raging torrent that she couldn't stop, and she couldn't afford to give way, not now, not here. Maybe when she got to England?

She lay back on the bed and took some long deep breaths to calm her thudding heart. She would get through this. She had only known him a few weeks, after all; she couldn't, *wouldn't* let him mean anything to her. But it was too late, weeks too late.

She wasn't aware that she had fallen asleep but as the knock sounded at the bedroom door she came to with such a sudden jerk that it made her dizzy. Teresa. The little maid had returned for the tray. She glanced at the untouched food guiltily as she climbed off the bed and padded across to the small table, calling out a 'come in' as she went. 'I'm sorry, Teresa, I'm just not hungry,' she said as she swung round with the tray in her hands to see Francisco's tall, dark shape standing quietly leaning against the half-open door. It was only a pure reflex action that enabled her nerveless fingers to hold on to the tray and as she set it down again on the table, her hands shaking as she pulled the massive towel more tightly round her trembling body, the partially full wine glass rocked and shuddered before righting itself.

'I have booked you a seat on the first available flight to England, which is in forty-eight hours,' Francisco said thickly, his eyes on her hair, which had tumbled loose from the small hand-towel and fallen to curl in soft shining silver-blonde waves on her shoulders. 'I hope that is acceptable?'

'That's fine.' Every drop of her will-power was focused on keeping her body straight and still and her face calm. 'Thank you.'

'The ticket can be picked up at Reception when you arrive,' he continued formally, 'but Alfonso will explain all the details to you tomorrow.'

She nodded carefully, biting her lower lip hard to prevent the weakness that was settling on her body from showing on her face. 'I'll repay you for the fare once I get home,' she said quietly, forcing all emotion from her voice.

'That will not be necessary.'

'Necessary or not, I'd prefer it that way,' she said obstinately, her lip trembling before she could turn her face away from the rapier-sharp gaze.

'Lorne...' His face had whitened as the black eyes swept over her small face, and he took a step towards her, his arms reaching out for a brief moment before they fell back by his side and, turning abruptly, he left.

'I can't stand this.' As the door shut behind him she clasped her arms round her waist in an agony of blinding pain, shutting her eyes as she swayed to and fro in the silent room. Why was he torturing her like this? Why didn't he shout at her, scream, rage, anything...? Anything but this tight, unrelenting formality that was like a wall of rock between them.

'You must not let him send you away.' Rosa's words swam into her mind through the cloying blackness that was taking over her soul, and she suddenly longed for the small Spanish woman with an intensity that was as fierce as it was irrational. How could she stop him? She walked over to the bed and sat down carefully as though any sudden movement would break her into a million tiny pieces. How could anyone stop him doing anything? She had never met anyone, male or female, whose will was so inflexible, whose spirit was so strong. She couldn't reach him; no one could.

The night was endless. Halfway through the interminable vigil she wandered outside to the shadowed balcony, sitting quietly in the velvet darkness that was warm and soft on her skin. She couldn't cry any more, the sense of loss was too deep for tears, and it didn't help to tell herself, over and over again, that one couldn't miss what one had never had.

She didn't know at what point she became aware of another presence on the veranda below; it was a gradual realisation that crept up on her senses in spite of the utter stillness of the night. And she knew it was him. The thought should have brought some comfort, an easing to her pain, but instead she found she was suffering for his misery as well as her own as she sat there in the thick blackness. When she could think of him as being heartless, ruthless, cold, it went some way to blanketing the agony from her mind, but when, as now, she recognised her intuitive instinct for feeling the tearing anguish she had perceived in him time and time again, her own torment was doubled.

He was like a great black cat that walked alone
in a solitary desolate existence, asking for no
quarter and giving none, isolated and remote
from the normal human ups and downs of life.
Something was torturing him, eating away at him
each day with sharp, jagged teeth, but instead of
reaching out for comfort and seeking a way to
alleviate his suffering he was bearing it alone,
proud, aloof and piercingly cold.

The hours dragged on and still she was unable
to sleep until, as dawn sent its fingers of pink
into the night sky, she crept back to bed wearily.

The thud, light as it was, brought her from the
drowsy dullness her tired mind had taken refuge
in and she sat bolt upright in bed, her heart
thumping. The sound had seemed to come from
the balcony but there was a sheer wall under-
neath her window with no visible means of
climbing it.

What was the time? She glanced at her old
weathered wristwatch in the dim light. Five
o'clock in the morning. She had only been back
in bed for half an hour.

She padded over to the open doors of the
balcony warily, pulling the flimsy curtain aside
as she peered out into the warm morning air
already filled with the promise of another
scorchingly hot day. For a moment she saw
nothing and then a slight movement in the far
corner of the floor brought her eyes swinging to
the ground. It was a tiny little bird.

'Oh, no, oh, you poor thing.' The minute little
ball of fluff and feathers had clearly flown into

the unyielding window of the balcony and stunned itself and now it sat helplessly, tiny black eyes fixed unblinkingly on her face, as she walked across and knelt down by its side. It made no effort to fly away and as she cupped it in her hands the little body fell over sideways and lay looking up at her in bewildered confusion. 'What have you done to yourself?' she whispered softly. 'You don't look big enough to have left your mum.'

And then the tears came, hot, blinding tears that melted the last remnants of the shield she had tried to keep in place for so long. *She loved him.* In the same way this little scrap of life in her hands had flown into the cold glass and been knocked sideways by its inflexible, pitiless density she had flown into Francisco and suffered the same fate. That was why his pain was her pain, why each word spoken in anger had the power to send her to hell and back. And she had known all along, deep in the hidden recesses of her mind, right from that first day when he had rescued her and stormed the citadel of her heart. What was she going to do? She moaned softly as she still held the little bird tenderly in her hands. What could she do? Nothing.

She was still holding the tiny sparrow two hours later when Benita knocked on the door with her morning cup of tea, the little Spanish girl's eyes widening when Lorne explained what had happened and asked for a box.

'A box, *señorita*?' Benita stared at her as if she were mad. 'No, no box. You give me, I ...' She made a gesture of wringing her hands and Lorne moved back a pace in horror.

'I want a box,' she repeated angrily, 'and don't you dare lay a finger on this bird.'

This new side to Lorne was clearly something of a shock to Benita, who disappeared immediately without another word, her glance of scornful perplexity expressing her opinion of the proceedings far more adequately than any words could have done. 'It's a good job you didn't fly into *her* window,' Lorne whispered softly to the little face looking up at her so quietly. 'Just remember that next time you take an early morning stroll.' She couldn't bear the thought that the little thing might die. Suddenly the bird's fate had taken on an importance far beyond the normal concern she would have for any animal in a similar situation. It *had* to get better, *had* to carry on with its life; it couldn't give in and crumble. Its destiny was all mixed up with hers and for the moment she was incapable of separating the two.

When the door opened again behind her she spoke with unusual sharpness. 'I hope you've brought the box, Benita, and I'm keeping it with me.'

'Will this do?' Francisco's deep, soft voice made her jump so violently that she nearly dropped the bird, who looked up at her with wide, reproachful eyes. He placed a small box with layers of tissue paper at the bottom on the floor by her feet. 'Can I see?'

As she handed her tiny charge to him she glanced at his face for the first time and her heart caught painfully with the force of her love for him. He looked infinitely tired, the deep lines round his mouth and eyes seeming to be carved into the tanned skin as though by a knife. He was looking at the bird, not at her, and she allowed her eyes to feast on him for a long moment before dropping her gaze to the bundle of feathers in his large, capable hands. He was feeling the tiny body with expert precision, folding out first one minute wing, then another, his fingers deft and sure.

'Speaking as a doctor and not as a vet, I would say there are no obvious internal injuries,' he said quietly as he placed the tiny bird in the box with gentle fingers. 'It has probably just stunned itself for a while.'

'That's what I thought,' she agreed eagerly. 'It seems better than it was already.'

'How could it be otherwise when you are caring for it?' He straightened as he spoke to stand looking down at her from his great height with a strange expression tightening his face. 'I would suggest we leave it in peace for a little while longer and then after breakfast we can try letting it loose to find its companions. The sound of the other birds will perhaps draw it out of its shock.'

And what will draw *you* out? she asked silently as she nodded her agreement. What will make you break down this unscaleable wall that you've built round yourself so effectively? 'All right, after breakfast, then,' she agreed flatly as he walked to the door.

This was her last day. The thought was hammering in her mind as she showered and dressed mechanically, not even noticing what she put on. By tomorrow she would just be a memory for him—and for her? He would always be her love. If she couldn't have him she wouldn't have anyone else even if it meant a life alone. She glanced at her face in the mirror as she brushed her hair into sleek order, leaving it loose across her shoulders, its silky softness framing a face that was almost ghostly in its pallor. And it would mean just that because nothing, nothing could reach him.

She couldn't eat a thing at breakfast and she noticed Francisco only had several cups of black coffee. Immediately afterwards she fetched the box from her bedroom to find him waiting for her in the hall. He looked into the box silently, his fingers firm and compassionate as he lifted the tiny warm bundle of feathers and bright black eyes and walked carefully into the garden with Lorne at his side.

'It is down to you now, little one,' he said softly to the bird as it huddled in his hands before he crouched down to place the tiny body in the middle of the huge lawn where it stared at them both unblinkingly.

The sun was warm on her skin as she stood there in the quiet, scented air looking at the tall, powerful figure kneeling so tenderly by the minute shape of the tiny bird, and for a moment the contrast was so stirringly poignant that her bruised heart ached. He was worth loving, this man. Worth every tear, every painful sigh. The image he showed the world, the cold, cruel, ruthless tycoon with a love-'em-and-leave-'em approach to his women and hard, unbending attitude to the rest of the human race, that wasn't the real Francisco. She knew it as surely as she drew breath. She didn't know what had happened to cement the mask in place so firmly, perhaps she would never know, but it was a mask. This was the real man, caring, kind, tender and compassionate to anything weaker and frailer than himself. The very depth of his suffering was proof of his vulnerability.

She was so lost in thought that the sudden movement of the bird as it spread its wings and flew up into the wide blue sky almost caught her by surprise. 'It's gone.' She caught hold of Francisco's arm in her delight. 'It's all right.'

'Yes.' He smiled slowly at her pleasure and shaded his eyes as they followed the bird's swooping progress in the clear warm air. 'It just needed time, that's all.'

'And you?' She forced herself to face him. 'How much time do you need?'

'Me?' The smile died as he looked into the intense grey of her eyes. 'All the time in the world couldn't make it right for me, *infanta*; I only wish it could. I would like to fly again, free and clean and at peace.'

They stared at each other for a long, timeless moment and as her eyes filled with tears, turning luminous in the white sunlight, he caught her to him with a groan that seemed to be wrenched from his very soul. 'Don't look like that, don't care so much.' He was almost squeezing the breath from her body but she didn't care. 'You are young, you have your whole life before you. All this will mean nothing to you in a few months.'

'Don't say that!' She tore herself out of his arms. 'I'm not a child, Francisco.'

'I know that,' he said flatly.

'Then why won't you tell me what's wrong? Why can't you share it with me? I might be able to help,' she finished desperately.

'Help?' The sharp bark of a laugh was mirthless.

'You won't even consider talking to me, will you?' In spite of her love for him the anger was hot and fierce. 'You don't care about me, my feelings; you're so wrapped up in whatever it is that's hurt you, nothing else matters.'

'Of course you matter.' The words shot out like bullets. 'It is because you matter that I must be strong.'

'Strong?' She almost screamed the word at him. 'Oh, you're strong all right; I've never met anyone else in my life who is as "strong" if that's the right word! I'd rather use "stubborn", "dogged", "immovable", though, to be more precise.'

'I will not discuss this with you, Lorne, there is no point.'

'No point!' The cold control in his voice was the last straw. 'How can you say that to me?'

'I say it because it is the truth,' he said grimly, his eyes stormy. 'You are a luxury I cannot afford, Lorne. I cannot allow myself to become weak.'

'Caring for someone doesn't make you weak,' she protested faintly, the hard glitter of the jet-black eyes chilling her bones.

He shrugged slowly, his face set in granite. 'We must agree to differ on this as in most things,' he said tightly. 'You speak with the voice of youth and hope, I speak from experience. I will never permit a woman to impair my judgement again; the cost may be too high as it was in the past——' He stopped abruptly, obviously feeling he had said too much.

'In the past?' Even as she spoke he had left her to stride towards the house, his back straight and his shoulders taut. In the past? The words echoed in her mind as she sank down on to the sun-warmed grass rich with the scent of a thousand summer days. What did that mean? A woman had been involved in this thing that haunted him? She shut her eyes against the white light as her brain buzzed on. But it wasn't a simple betrayal or something along those lines— he would have risen above that. So what? The sick feeling in her chest grew as her mind explored a hundred possibilities. *He would send her away not knowing*. The panic in her rose like a live thing, clawing at her throat with stifling fingers.

She could ask Alfonso again. 'No.' She spoke out loud into the fresh morning air. Her

relationship with the old retainer had improved
dramatically over the last few weeks but he still
maintained a steadfast reticence on anything
slightly personal relating to his master, and she
knew he had instructed both the maids to say
nothing to her. She couldn't embarrass them by
asking pertinent questions. Rosa? But there was
no way she could go and visit the little housekeeper even if she could find her way back to the
villa, which she couldn't. It was hopeless.

Francisco was in his study when she went back
to the house, the door firmly closed, and, after
spending a miserable half an hour in her room
with her mind churning on until she felt as though
she could scream, she decided to go for a swim.

The water was clean and silky to the touch and
she drove herself to cover twenty lengths without
stopping before climbing out to lie on one of the
comfortable sun-loungers. The sky was a brilliant
blue, the surroundings beautiful, and yet there
was a greyness colouring her soul that made
everything dull. How long would she feel like
this? She stretched back on the warm cushions,
shutting her eyes after spreading out her wet hair
fan-like to dry in the hot sun. The caressing heat
on her water-cooled skin, the slow drone of tiny
insects from the vegetation all around and the
effects of the violent exercise after a sleepless
night all worked their toll on her nervous system,
and she drifted off into a deep sleep without being
aware of it.

The sixth sense that had served her in the past
brought her instantly awake some time later and

as her grey eyes opened wide they fixed on Francisco as he lay at her side, the dark brown eyes open and unguarded as he watched her while she slept. She caught her breath at the naked hunger and pain she read in his gaze seconds before the shutter came down and hid his expression from her.

'You were tired.' He shifted his position on his sun-lounger as he spoke, turning over on to his back and shutting his eyes quickly after slipping on a pair of dark sunglasses.

'I didn't sleep much last night.' The time for false pride had long since gone, she decided firmly. 'Did you?'

He hesitated for a long moment before replying and then his voice was reluctant. 'No.'

'What time is my flight tomorrow?'

This time the silence was even longer.

'Early afternoon,' he said at last, his voice so expressionless that it was an admission of emotion in itself.

'Are you coming to see me off?' she asked carefully.

'Lorne——' He moved so violently that she almost fell off her sun-lounger. 'What are you trying to do to me?' He sat up, the sunglasses still rigidly in place, but although his eyes were hidden from her the small muscle that clenched at the side of the square jaw spoke volumes. 'You want blood, is that it?'

'Blood?' She kept her voice calm although the surge of fierce excitement that flooded through her body was rivetingly hot. This was the first

time he had intimated that he would find the
parting painful. 'I don't know what you mean,
Francisco. I just wondered if you were coming
to the airport with me.'

The dark shades stared at her blankly for a full
minute before he turned away, pulling off the
short-sleeved cotton shirt and jeans he was
wearing before tossing the glasses on to the heap
of discarded clothes as he walked to the pool's
tiled edge and dived in. As the powerful shoulders
cut through the water in a pounding rhythm that
was pure aggression she watched him shakily. The
dynamic energy was almost tangible.

She envied those women who had shared his
bed; at least they had memories to keep them
warm at night... She sliced into her thoughts with
a ruthlessness he would have been proud of. She
would not allow herself to think like this or allow
those pangs of raw jealousy to bite into her soul.
But she *wanted* him to remember her. The tears
that were ever ready these days pricked hot
against the back of her eyes.

As he pulled himself out of the water the magnificent body drew her eyes like a magnet. Those
few times she had been in his arms had told her
he would be a breathtakingly sensual lover and
she didn't doubt he was an expert in the diverse
arts of love. Why did he want her? She stared at
him as he walked towards her. Was it just because she was something new, her innocence a
novelty to the worldly-wise, cynical man he had
become? Probably. Her heart jarred and then
pounded violently. He had never said anything

to suggest his desire was anything else but physical, after all, and now there was no time left. The sand in the hour-glass that he had talked about had all but run out.

'I am not sure if the expression on your face is a compliment or otherwise,' he said laconically as he flung himself down on the sun-lounger next to hers, a few drops of water from his wet skin splashing on to hers. 'I only know it makes me want to take you right here and now.' The enigmatic mask was firmly in place, she noted wryly as hot colour flooded her face scarlet. He was wearing the same brief swimming-trunks as before and suddenly there didn't seem a safe place to fix her eyes.

'Do you have any idea, any idea at all, just how lovely you are?' he asked thickly before turning over face down on the lounger, his head turned away from her.

Not lovely *enough*, obviously, she thought painfully, or perhaps slim, small blondes just weren't his type? If she had been tall, perhaps a sultry redhead or vivacious brunette, would that have found a chink in the steel-hard armour? She lay back on the cushions and shut her eyes again. There were too many ifs and buts featuring in her thoughts these days. He wanted her, but not so badly that he was prepared to do anything about it. That was the bottom line and it was time to face it.

She must have fallen asleep again because the next thing she knew Teresa and Benita had arrived to serve them lunch by the pool.

'Eat,' Francisco said quietly when they were seated under one of the huge striped umbrellas with a full plate in front of them. 'You did not eat a thing at breakfast.'

'Neither did you,' she returned quickly.

'This is so.' He nodded gravely and her heart gave a little jump. Why did he have to be so handsome, so darned overwhelmingly attractive? 'We will now both rectify our failings, *sí*? And after lunch I must work in my study but you will have dinner with me tonight? You do not intend to hide in your room?'

'I've never hidden in my room,' she said with more vehemence than truth. He raised dark eyebrows in disbelief as he poured her a glass of deep-red wine from the opened bottle at his side, but said nothing.

She stayed by the pool all afternoon, alternating between swimming and dozing in the thick warm air, and felt rested in her body if not her mind when she wandered back to the house as dusk began to fall. The uninterrupted hours in the sun had given her already tanned skin a soft honey glow and she washed her hair more carefully than usual, smoothing a rich conditioner into the thick blonde strands that, once dried, swirled round her shoulders like gleaming silk. She *had* to look good tonight. She gazed at her reflection in the mirror as she made good use of Catalina's cosmetics, smoothing a moisturiser into her smooth, clear skin and applying a touch of gold eyeshadow to her lids. She decided against foundation—the sun's natural glow had given her skin a warm tint that no artificial gloss could complement.

The choice of evening wear was a little more complicated, due to Catalina being a few inches taller than her, but she eventually found a sleeveless top in gold silk cut like a small waistcoat that fitted her perfectly, along with a swirling black skirt that she imagined was a mini on Francisco's sister but came to just above her knees. She was sitting gazing regretfully at her old black pumps, which didn't fit in at all well with the general theme of elegant sophistication, when Teresa knocked quietly at her door. 'The *señor*, he ready, Señorita Lorne,' she said softly as she came into the room.

'Thanks, Teresa.' As Lorne raised her eyes the small maid glanced at the worn shoes sitting by her feet, her brown eyes widening in sudden comprehension.

'*Señorita*, I have the sandals that may fit.' She indicated her own small feet by way of explanation. 'You like to try maybe?'

'There's no maybe about it.' Lorne nodded eagerly. 'Yes, please, Teresa, these old shoes of mine have just about had it.'

When Teresa returned two minutes later she was holding small low-heeled sandals in the exact gold of the waistcoat which fitted perfectly, along with a pair of pretty little gold earrings in the shape of tiny fans which she gave to Lorne with a pleased smile. 'You have for this night,' she said firmly. 'Is the birthday present from my father, *sí*?'

'That's so nice of you.' Lorne totally confused the small maid by hugging her impulsively before turning to fit the delicate jewellery into her ears. 'How do I look?'

'Very pretty, *señorita*.' Teresa drew the first word out in rapturous approval. 'And now the *señor*, he waits for you.'

'I'm ready.' As they left the room Lorne felt her heart thud up into her mouth. She was stupid, *stupid* to hope she could get through to him, but she was pinning all her hopes on this last evening. Where was her pride? The thought jarred in her head as she walked carefully down the long winding staircase. In ashes at his feet, came the reply.

The look in his eyes as she joined him was reward enough for all the effort. 'You look quite beautiful,' he said softly, his warm gaze lingering on her lips just long enough for her to feel thoroughly kissed. 'A princess indeed.'

She'd settle for ordinary plain commoner if he went along with it, she thought wryly as he bent over her hand with a little bow. His lips were warm and firm on the back of her hand and as he turned her fingers over and kissed the soft flesh of her palm in a slowly sensual caress that caused every nerve-ending in her body to sing into glorious life she stared down at his bent head with that feeling of indescribable panic taking hold of her again. She couldn't just walk out of his life, could she? He wouldn't let her...would he?

'And now we go.' As he straightened she saw he was smiling.

'Go?' she asked bewilderedly. 'I thought we were going to have dinner.'

'And so we are.' He took her elbow firmly and guided her towards the door. 'In a little place I know.'

'But——'

'I want our last night together to be special.' The words cut through her like a knife and she was glad he had just ushered her in front of him as he opened the door leading on to the darkened drive because her face froze for a brief moment.

She was thankful she had taken such care with her toilette as the powerful car ate up the miles on the unlit black roads. He was devastating in what looked like the same black velvet dinner-jacket he had worn on that evening when he had rescued her, looking perfectly groomed and with an air of fierce inherent sexuality that made her hands damp and her stomach warm.

'Our last night together'. The words were pounding in her head as the soft, sexy music from the car stereo filtered through her senses. This was just a last magnanimous gesture as far as he was concerned, a little treat so that the whole miserable episode ended well and he could dismiss her tomorrow with an easy conscience. He didn't care about her, not really, not deep down in his soul. *And she loved him*. She took a long shuddering breath and stared straight ahead through the windscreen into the dark, shadowed night outside. Well, that was her misfortune and she would have to learn to live with it. She closed her eyes for a brief moment as her stomach somersaulted. He hadn't asked her to love him; in fact everything he had done had been to point her in the opposite direction. She had no one to blame but herself.

'It is not far now. Are you hungry?' His accent twisted her heart and as she gave a banal reply her mind chugged on. No other man would ever affect her like him; he was too hard an act to follow. Why hadn't she seen it, protected herself? But it had been too late from the first moment she had laid eyes on him.

'There, up on the hill. You see the lights?'

As she came out of her reverie it was to see a mass of flickering, diamond-bright lights in the distance like tiny stars in a dark silky sky. 'It looks very grand,' she said doubtfully as the dim outline of a huge building took shape.

'It is,' he said quietly, a thread of hidden amusement in the deep voice. 'And there will not be one person present who is worthy to clean your shoes.' The tenor of his voice had altered, softened. 'They are just ordinary people, Lorne, with the same failings and faults common to the rest of us, but you, you are my *infanta*. Do not allow yourself to think that these folk are better than you.'

How could he *say* things like that and still send her away? she thought helplessly. What went on in that hard, razor-sharp mind anyway?

The hotel was surrounded by exquisitely land-scaped gardens lit with hundreds of concealed lights that gave the carefully positioned shrubs and trees maximum effect, and as they drove into

the huge central courtyard where cars worthy to
be considered companions to Francisco's Ferrari
were parked with regal poise she silently blessed
the absent Catalina with an added postscript to
Teresa.

The interior of the palatial building did justice
to the lead-up, and as she walked through the
ankle-deep cream carpet into the ornately
decorated dining-room she felt as though she was
in another world. His world. A world of spec-
tacularly casual wealth, attentive and deferential
waiters and fabulous, beautiful surroundings.
How could she ever have hoped such a man
would want her? But she *was* as good as anyone
here. The obstinate streak she had inherited from
her father rose to the fore. As Francisco had said,
they were just ordinary folk. The flashing dia-
monds and furs and silks covered bodies that were
just as vulnerable as hers with hearts that could
break just as easily.

'Señor de Vega...' Someone who must be the
head waiter descended on Francisco with a burst
of incomprehensible Spanish and they were
shown to a secluded table for two with great cer-
emony, which Francisco seemed quite unaware
of and which made Lorne want to curl up and
die with embarrassment.

'A champagne cocktail while we decide what
to eat?' Francisco eyed her smilingly as the waiter
still hovered at their side.

'Fine.' She managed a cool smile.

By the time she had drunk the cocktail and
surveyed her surroundings Lorne found her

heartbeat was returning to normal, and when the meal came, a veritable masterpiece of culinary delight, two more cocktails had relaxed her sufficiently to eat with slow appreciation. Francisco was humorous, relaxed and lazily enigmatic, and she knew with absolute certainty that he was acting a part. She didn't know how she knew— perhaps it was her love for him that made her sensitive to every tiny flicker of his eyes, every expression—but she knew none the less that another mask had been brought out and donned for the occasion.

'What do you plan to do once you are home?' he asked softly as they finished a dessert that was all chocolate, cream and calories.

'I don't know.' She lowered her head as she idly swept her finger round the rim of the expensively cut crystal wine glass. 'Get a job, I suppose, maybe spend a little time with Tom and the kids. I don't know.'

'Will you come back to Spain again?'

She raised her head then to look him straight in the eyes, her mouth tight. 'Do you want me to?'

He stared back at her for a long moment as something worked in his face she couldn't read. 'I didn't mean... I wasn't asking——' He stopped abruptly. 'Or maybe I was. Hell, I think I do not know what I am trying to say to you, Lorne.'

The momentary loss of composure pleased her more than words could say but she kept silent, her eyes on his face. It had to come from him; she had played all her cards.

'I have something for you, a memento to remember this time in your life by.' She noticed he didn't say to remember him by and also that he had very adroitly cut the thread of the conversation without any embarrassment to either of them. He was very good at this, she thought wryly, she had to give him that, but maybe he had had a lot of practice?

'What is it?' She took the small box he placed in her hands warily. He had done so much for her already, she couldn't accept—— 'Oh, it's beautiful.' As she stared at the tiny little fairy-tale castle worked in fine glass she saw the minute little gold figure at the top of the tower.

'A castle for a princess,' he said slowly, 'where she can wait in safety for her knight to come and rescue her.' He remembered that early conversation, she thought bemusedly as she examined the intricate thread-like structure. 'You deserve the best, my *infanta*, do not accept anything less. You will not be seeing this Sancho?'

'No.' The strength of purpose she felt in him frightened her and a cold shiver flickered down her spine. He was so sure of himself, so unbending.

'This is good,' he said grimly. 'It will save me having to find him and persuade him that he is no good for you.'

'I wouldn't let you do that,' she began indignantly. 'You've got no right——'

'Please, let us not discuss this.' He took her hand in his and she shivered again but this time with the darting pleasure his touch evoked. 'I want this thing to end well.'

'Why does it have to end?' She shouldn't be saying this, she thought desperately; it would do no good. 'Can't you tell me what's wrong, trust me a little——?'

'Enough.' His voice was hard now and his face closed as he removed his hand from hers. 'This is just a brief interlude in your life, Lorne. You will soon forget me; you are young——'

'I'll hit you if you mention my age again,' she said fiercely as hot tears stung the back of her eyes. 'I won't forget you, don't you see? You aren't being fair——'

His face took on the cold formality that dried up the words in her throat more adequately than his anger could have done, and she subsided back into her seat with a little soundless moan. She had lost, totally and completely. He was a man of ice, hard and unyielding, and he didn't even know he had taken her heart.

## CHAPTER NINE

THE drive home was sheer torture. In spite of Francisco's cold silence and stiff profile Lorne could feel the dark vital blackness emanating from his very being as though it were tangible.

She should never have said anything, she told herself bitterly, only to correct herself the next second. Yes, she should, she *damn well should*! She couldn't play games, pretend to be something she wasn't; she had to say what was in her heart and if he didn't like it—— And he obviously hadn't. She darted a sly glance at the austere outline of his face in the car's dim interior and her heart lurched frantically. The sand had all gone. It was finished, over.

He said a polite goodnight once they were home but she could feel his eyes on the back of her head as she walked slowly up the long winding staircase to her room. 'Francisco?' She stopped halfway and turned to meet his gaze and again, in that brief unguarded moment, saw an agonised hunger that stunned her. 'Will I see you again before I go?'

'Lorne...' It seemed as though he dragged his eyes from her face with a pain that cut through his whole body. 'I cannot talk to you now. Go to bed.'

163

She stumbled into her room on legs that trembled violently, standing for a long minute in front of the full-length mirror as she tried to look at herself dispassionately, to see what he would see. She had gone out with such high hopes tonight; she could admit it now it was all over. She had thought the force of her love was too strong, too fierce, not to break through his iron reserve, that such an intensity of emotion must spark some answering chord in him. 'You are so stupid,' she told the misty reflection slowly as her dazed eyes criticised the small slender shape under its mass of blonde hair. 'What would he see in you?' She left the beautiful clothes in a discarded pile on the floor as she went into the bathroom, turning the flow of water on to its fullest pitch so that the tiny needles pricked against her skin as she stood under the torrential cascade. She stood under there for a long time until she had gained control of her emotions. She couldn't enjoy the luxury of tears; she had already decided that would have to wait until she got home to England because if she once opened the floodgates she would never stop.

She slipped into a thick, fleecy robe, knotting the belt tightly round her waist as she began to dry her hair slowly, and as the quiet knock sounded at the door she glanced at her watch quickly. It was past midnight. Surely Teresa hadn't come at this time of night for her sandals and earrings?

'Lorne?' The voice outside the door certainly wasn't Teresa's. 'I want to talk to you; can I come in?'

'Francisco?' She flew to the door and opened it jerkily, her eyes wide as she looked up into the shadowed darkness of his face. 'What is it?'

'I need to be with you tonight.' The lost, desperate look on his face cut into her like a knife. 'I thought I was strong enough to get through but I am going crazy, *pequeña*.' He shook his head like a prize-fighter after the knock-out blow. 'Can I come in? I just want to hold you in my arms, to wake up beside you in the morning, that is all, nothing more.'

'Francisco...' She took his hand and led him into the bedroom in much the same way as she would have done with a child, shutting the door behind her before turning and flinging herself into the arms that opened instinctively to receive her.

'I will not take your innocence,' he said again as he held her to him so tightly that the breath left her body. 'It would not be fair when I can give you nothing more.'

'Why can't you?' She moved back slightly to look up into his face, seeing the lines of strain about his mouth and eyes with deep compassion. 'Why can't you just give us a chance? I'm not asking that you declare undying love immediately or say you've been waiting for me all your life. I know you don't love me but there's an attraction between us, isn't there?' She stared up at him, her soft grey eyes enormous with uncorscious pleading. 'There's something...isn't there?'

'Yes, there is something.' He pushed her away gently as he moved back a pace, his black eyes bleak.

'Well, then?' She held out her hands in a little lost gesture.

'I have to tell you, I can see that now.' He seemed to be speaking to himself and she hardly dared breathe as the dark gaze moved back to her face. 'Sit down, Lorne.' He gestured towards the bed. 'And let me tell you this in my own way.'

'What is it?' She stiffened with fear. He was going to tell her there was someone else after all? A wife maybe, a sweetheart?

'You know about the accident?' She nodded slowly. 'How much do you know, really know, Lorne?'

She swallowed painfully as the panic still clawed at her throat. 'Only what I said that day. That the yacht caught fire and lots of people were killed.'

'Lots of people.' He nodded grimly, his face suddenly gaunt. 'Yes. My mother died that day, along with my brother and his wife and their three children, Alfonso's wife and three other people, one of whom was a businessman who had come to dinner to talk about a proposed merger, a very important proposed merger. At that point I was officially head of the family, my father having died two years before.'

'Yes?' She stared at him bewilderedly. What did all this have to do with them now?

'I had made the arrangements for Señor Malveños to dine on the yacht; I thought the obvious display of wealth would impress him, make the business all that more easier.' His mouth had twisted in such a grimace of self-contempt that she almost flew across to his side but controlled herself just in time. She was trembling now, a despair taking hold of her that sent icy trickles down her spine. Whatever this was it had devastated him. 'And then, at the last minute, I asked my brother to stand in for me with his wife acting as hostess. I described it as good experience for him and a little treat for his children. It had been some time since they had slept on the yacht. He agreed immediately but then he always did; he was one of the most affable men I have ever met.'

'Francisco——'

'No, let me finish.' He held up his hand quickly. 'My mother decided she would like to go and help take care of the children in case they should prove troublesome; one of them was teething, if I remember rightly. Anyway, she always could make an excuse to be with them; she adored them. And so they all set off; I actually waved them goodbye from the front steps when they came to pick Mother up. I had told them I had an important appointment it was imperative to keep and they trusted me without further explanation. And six hours later they were dead.'

He drew a shaking hand over his face which was grey and wet with sweat. 'It was two o'clock in the morning when Alfonso telephoned the number I had left for emergencies. He woke me up and told me, very gently, what had happened. I listened, I put down the receiver, and then I glanced at the woman by my side. The woman I had been bedding. Not the love of my life, you understand.' His voice was bitterly cutting. 'Just an available and very attractive socialite who had made it clear that her favours were on offer. And because of my...' his lips had curled away from his teeth in a devil's mask '...appetite, ten people had died horrifying deaths. And it was horrifying, Lorne. I will not distress you with the details but some of them lived for a few minutes and death was a merciful release.'

Her face was ashen as her eyes remained locked on his. 'Oh, my poor love.' She wasn't aware she had spoken out loud until his voice cut into the space between them like a whip.

'You can say that? Do you not despise me? Do you not feel disgust for such a man as I? You had thought I was noble? I could see it in your every glance—but I am less than human, you see it now?'

'No, I don't see that,' she whispered into the agonised silence, his face a blur through the tears pouring down her cheeks. 'I see a man with a heart so big it has almost killed him. A man who cannot forgive himself for something that was not his fault, who is punishing himself beyond the limit any human being can endure.'

'But I have to be alive to do that.' She thought, from the thickness of his voice and what she could see of his face through her tears, that his own cheeks were wet. 'I was brought up, as the elder son, to put duty first at all times. I re-affirmed that responsibility to my father on his deathbed and in the betrayal of his trust I wiped out his whole family. If I suffer the torments of hell endlessly it still will not be enough. Three children, Lorne...' His voice broke in a groan of despair. 'I went mad for a time afterwards.'

'Is that when you went to the cottage?' she whispered slowly.

'*Sí.*' He shook his head helplessly. 'Rosa and Josef, they saved my sanity along with Alfonso and Teresa. In spite of their own pain they never once blamed me.'

'And they were right, don't you see?' She went to him now, tiny and slender against his bulk as he stood rigidly in the centre of the room. 'It was an accident, just an accident. It could have hap-pened the next week, the next month, when you were on board and not them, but it didn't, it happened that night. It was terrible, wickedly cruel, but no more your fault than theirs. And now you have to deal with it, to put it behind you. Do you think they would have wanted you to die with them? Because that's what you've done to all intents and purposes. It makes their deaths even more pointless——'

'You do not understand——'

'Don't you say that to me! Don't you dare say that!' She had thrown the words into his face with the vehemence of her love and a breathtakingly tight silence pervaded the room as they faced each other silently. 'Do you think you're the only person who can feel pain, feel regret, is that it?' Her voice was low and soft and agonised. 'Well, I've lost loved ones and I *know* how it feels. That day my parents were killed I'd had a row with my father over something, I can't even remember what now, and instead of kissing him goodbye as he wanted I'd stayed sulking in my room. That was a hard thing to come to terms with for a ten-year-old child, Francisco. I'm not saying I felt as bad as you, I don't know, but don't tell me I don't understand. And I mean what I said. If it had been you that had died, and your brother was in your place, would you have wanted him to throw his life away? He loved you, he would want you to learn to live with your grief and try to understand that it was just fate, destiny, call it what you will.'

'I cannot accept that. His voice was dead-sounding. 'I have no right to be alive but alive I am and as long as I live I will do my duty.'

'Your duty?' She took his arms urgently, feeling the muscles tense beneath her touch. 'Your duty to them means trying to be happy again, don't you see? Don't you see how pointless you're making their deaths? You think they died for you, which isn't true, but even if you do think that for you to bury yourself in this way makes it all so...' Her voice trailed away as she searched for a word adequate to express her pain.

'Pointless?' he asked expressionlessly. 'I know what you are trying to say, *pequeña*, and I am not ungrateful but——'

'Damn your buts!' She actually shook him in her desperation. She wasn't getting through. 'Open up your mind, Francisco, break out of that prison you've made for yourself. Ask for absolution.'

'I do not have the right.' He turned to go, his face ashen. 'And I should not have involved you in this; I should just have let you go.'

'Don't say that.' As he walked to the door panic and shock had her flying after him. 'Francisco!' She caught hold of his arms again, her face frantic. 'Don't go, not like this. I want——'

'You cannot make it all right, do you not see?' He looked down at her with something like compassion on his dark face. 'We have to live with the consequences of our actions and I am no different from anyone else.'

'I could help——'

'Lorne, I dare not take the chance that I would pull you down with me.' He tried to loosen her hands but she clung on all the tighter. 'Everything seems so simple with you but it could all go badly wrong——'

'I'm prepared to take that chance.' Her hands were like clamps on his arms.

'Well, I am not.' The words were final. 'Goodnight, Lorne.'

'No! Don't go, not like this.' There was a note of horror in her voice. 'You can't.'

'Lorne——'

'No, *please*.' She clung on to him in an agony of fear. He was so rigid, so strong; how could she penetrate that hard mind? 'Stay with me tonight, but properly. Make love to me. Let's have just one night together if that is all there can be. I love you, Francisco, I can't bear you to go. What shall I do?'

As the sound of her voice died away to breathless sobbing she saw he was as white as a sheet, his eyes depthless. For a moment, a stunningly long moment, she thought she had reached him as a vivid play of emotions washed across the hard face in fierce succession, but then he shook his head slowly as that mask she so feared settled in place over the handsome features.

'What you have just told me makes it even more impossible for me to stay,' he said gently. 'I had not realised that you felt so strongly, that you had imagined...' He loosened her grip with firm, cool hands and she found she had no strength to protest. 'I will not have the destruction of another life on my conscience.'

'Francisco!' As he turned to walk to the door her tortured cry stopped him for one breathtaking moment but then he moved forward, opening the door without glancing round and shutting it quietly behind him, and it seemed to her in that moment that all the colour, all the joy she would ever know had gone with him.

She sank down on to the carpet as her legs buckled beneath her, realising for the first time that she was weeping soundlessly, hopelessly, the tears cascading from her eyes, her nose in a drowning flood.

It was a long, long time before she could pull herself together sufficiently to wipe her face and blow her nose, and then she lay on the bed in the stillness of the night praying for a release from the pain that was a physical ache in her chest. Well, now she knew. She stared into the blackness blindly. But instead of providing the key to his heart her new knowledge had only made her realise how hopeless it all was. She loved him. She would *always* love him, but they would live their lives apart. She would leave here and he would stay. For a moment the realisation that he would be in the world, living, breathing, eating, sleeping and all without her was almost too much. And he would eventually marry. His choice would be made coldly and logically and with the sole motive of pursuing the commitment to duty. He would consider it necessary to provide future heirs and continue the family name and so it would be done.

She twisted deep in the throes of tormenting misery. She couldn't bear to see him again. Once the thought had been given life it cemented itself firmly in the forefront of her mind. Whether he said goodbye here or at the airport it would be equally impossible. She wouldn't be able to stand it. He would be cold and distant and aloof behind the barrier he had perfected in the last eight years and she would die... She sat up suddenly, her face burning and sore from the scalding tears and her throat dry. She would have to leave before morning.

She went about her preparations almost mechanically, glad to have something to do. She had a shower first and washed her hair, feeling better physically if not mentally once the stickiness of her tears had been washed away and the cool water had soothed her overheated skin.

It didn't take her long to pack her old rucksack. She put on her own T-shirt and shorts before stuffing the spare things she had brought with her from England into the canvas bag along with her passport and toilet bag. It felt strange to be in her own clothes again after the luxurious feel of Catalina's wildly expensive wardrobe.

'First mistake, girl,' she muttered to herself grimly as she brushed her hair with long savage strokes. 'You were in danger of forgetting yourself there for a while.'

Once she was ready to go she sat cross-legged on the bed looking out at the night sky. She couldn't go in pitch-blackness, she would have to wait until the first glimmer of dawn, but she forced her mind to empty itself with rigid determination. She couldn't afford to crack now and if she thought about Francisco and the agony he had revealed she would never make it, knowing that he wouldn't allow her to help, wouldn't accept any human comfort. Why couldn't he have loved her? She shut her eyes tightly for a long second as her heart pounded. They could have worked it out then, somehow. Was she doing the right thing in leaving like this? As the hours ticked by a hundred doubts filled her mind but then, as the first tentative streaks of pink ventured into the sky, she knew she had no choice. Whatever it took to say goodbye to him face to face she didn't have and somehow the thought of being carried from him screaming wasn't exactly agreeable.

She couldn't believe it once she was out in the grounds. Somehow, all through the stealthy creeping down the creaking winding stairs, she had expected lights to go on somewhere and somebody to challenge her. No, not expected...hoped. She shook her head in the chilly morning air as she walked briskly down the drive, her rucksack sitting on her back comfortably.

What was the time? Half-past four. She looked up at the dark sky thoughtfully. Teresa or Benita normally brought her a cup of tea about half-past seven but they might assume she was in her bathroom. Anyway, she'd cover as much distance as she could and hopefully reach the road and thumb a lift before the house really came to life.

It took her longer than she expected even to get out of the grounds and she realised she had miscalculated the swiftness of Francisco's Ferrari in comparison to her legs, and by the time she was halfway through the sweet-smelling pine forest, walking along the lane-like road that was sheltered and cool, the sun was already climbing in a glass-blue sky that promised fierce heat later. As the perfume of resinous bark and the chattering of the birds overhead in the high, straight branches lulled her into an easy rhythm she checked her watch again anxiously. She wanted to reach the main road by seven to catch the odd commuter who might be travelling to Extremadura or one of the other nearby towns on business. It might be ages before someone came along and even then would they stop for a rather bohemian-looking waif of a girl?

When she emerged on the other side of the pine forest the heat immediately struck her although it was still early in the morning. She pulled the old battered cloth hat she had bought on her first day in Spain out of the rucksack, looking at the creased material bemusedly. The girl who had laughed with Janie as they had tried on hat after hat while Sancho and Steve looked on and applauded was dead and gone. She remembered the humiliation and hurt she had felt a few days later when Sancho had deserted her and could have cried for the child she had been then. And she had been a child. In spite of all that had happened to her in her life up to that point it hadn't really touched the deep inner core that was hopeful and defiant, brave and determined, utterly sure that she could succeed at anything if she tried hard enough. And now? She pulled the hat over her fair hair brusquely. Now she knew better.

She heard the Ferrari before she saw it and had to force herself to turn and look, hoping desperately that it wasn't his car. The only vehicle that had passed her had been a broken-down old jeep loaded with a middle-aged Spanish couple and what looked like at least a dozen children piled into every available inch of space. They had smiled and waved and she had smiled and waved back and then she had been alone again, on the long, dusty road that seemed to stretch into infinity.

The blur of red in the distance confirmed her worst fears and the blood sang in her ears so fast that she almost missed her footing. That would be just great, she thought with painful humour, to collapse in front of him twice. Why had he followed her? To make sure she caught the plane? She had decided last night that she would make her own way home, work for some time some-where if necessary to pay for the ticket. She could pick fruit, wait at tables, anything. Or maybe this sense of duty had forced him to go the extra mile and make sure she was all right? Well, she was! She gritted her teeth as the car drew nearer. She was fine, *just fine*.

She saw the dark figure behind the steering-wheel just as the car screeched to a swirling stop, scattering red dust in a massive cloud that seemed to block out the sun for a brief moment, and her heart pounded so violently that she felt sick. She hadn't wanted to see him again and certainly not like this.

'What the hell, *what the hell* do you think you are doing now?' He had left the car almost before it stopped, leaving the door swinging open as he marched to her side, his face dark with furious rage. 'What is it with you, anyway? Do you have brainstorms, is that it?'

'Don't shout at me.' She glared back at him as she tried to stop shaking.

'Don't shout at you?' The incredulous note in his voice was echoed in the glazed ebony eyes. 'You tell me not to shout at you when you leave my house in the middle of the night to tramp about the countryside in the dark? You are insane, girl, insane or incredibly, wantonly stupid.'

The control had gone. She noted that with a curious kind of numb detachment as he hovered over her, almost demented in his fury.

'Have you any idea of what could happen to you out here all alone, of the pictures I have had in my mind since Teresa found you gone?' He shook her so violently that her head snapped back and the hat rolled into the dust at her feet, her hair spilling over her face in a mass of blonde waves. 'Do you?'

'I don't care!' Now she was shouting as she wrenched herself out of his hold, her eyes blazing. 'I don't care any more and what's it to you, anyway? You don't want me, you're not responsible for me, I didn't ask you to come and find me.'

'Stop this, Lorne.' His voice was calmer now as her own fury mounted, a burning-hot rage flooding her chest until she literally saw red.

'Why, why should I?' She knew she was making the alpha and omega of a fool of herself but the shock of seeing him again combined with his harsh words had temporarily robbed her of all constraint. 'I have the right to shout at you if I want to; I love you!' There was a logic in it somewhere although she couldn't have explained it herself. 'I'll always love you and you're making me go away. I hate you!'

'Lorne!' She knew she was on the edge of hysteria as he took her in his arms again, folding her against his chest in an iron hold that held her body captive in a rigid embrace. 'Calm down, you will make yourself ill.'

They stood unmoving for long minutes, his chin resting on the top of her head, and slowly her heartbeat stopped its furious racing and the explosion of rage died.

'You may think you love me, Lorne.' His voice was soft now and gentle. 'But you are very young and very beautiful. You will meet someone else who is able to love you as you should be loved. Someone of your own age who can laugh with you in the sunshine with no shadows to darken your life——'

'And that's it?' She pulled herself away to look up into the face she loved so dearly and wanted to slap so badly. 'I could hit you, Francisco, I really could. How can you write me off like that, as though I'm a child that, when deprived of one toy, can take up another? If you want me to agree with you, to make it better for you to go your own way and be miserable in peace, then you can forget it. I shan't meet anyone else, I don't have the choice any more, don't you see? From the moment I met you all my options dried up.'

He was staring at her as though he had never seen her before, his mouth half-open and his eyes wide.

'If I could have chosen for all that happened to you not to happen I would, as much for my own sake as yours, I admit, because now it's *my* pain, *my* agony because you're suffering it. Of course I'd rather have met a man with no skeletons in the cupboard but I didn't, I met you, and I can only love you. I don't care any more whether you believe that or not. I'm going now.'

She had turned and walked away so suddenly that it was a second or two before he realised what she was doing, and as she felt him behind her she made the gesture to run but it was too late. He lifted her, struggling and fighting now, into his arms and carried her towards the open car.

'Put me down, damn you!' She was crying again but in the face of all she had said the loss of a little more pride seemed trifling. 'I can look after myself.'

'I do not wish you to look after yourself, *infanta*.' As he placed her in the front seat all resistance ebbed out of her body in an exhausted flood, and she laid her head on the elegant dashboard and wept as though her heart would break. She didn't fight him as he cradled her against him, since it was probably the last time he would ever do so after all, but for a moment the feeling was so poignant that she didn't think she could bear it.

'You are very wrong, you know.' As she raised her face to look at him he shook his head slightly at the look of outrage on her face. 'I do not mean about the depth of your feelings for me, but about mine for you. You said last night that you knew I did not love you, that you wanted us to have a chance to see how we felt. But I loved you from the moment I picked you up off this road, *infanta*. Why do you think I could not let you go? I blessed that ankle for giving me the excuse I needed to keep you with me. I would have found another if you had not been injured but it would have been harder. It was unfair to you, criminally unfair, but I could not do the decent thing and let you go. I kept telling myself I would work up to it, another day, another week . . .' His voice trailed away into a deep hard groan. 'You deserve so much more. This blackness in me——'

'In us.' She placed her fingers on his lips as a relief so piercingly intense made her head swim. 'Don't you see? *In us*. You can share this thing now, bring it into the light of day. It will make it easier to bear, Francisco, I promise you.'

'And if it does not?' His eyes were haunted with a thousand images. 'Have you thought of that? It is one thing to be with someone because you care for them, because you want to be there, but what if this thing is bigger than both of us? I cannot promise to forget what has happened, Lorne; it is not possible.'

'I know that.' She bent her head back to look deep into his face. 'But we'll get through together even if we have to crawl every inch of the way. I shan't leave you, Francisco, whatever happens; I can't——'

'No.' He shook his head blindly. 'I want you to promise me that if things get too painful, too hard, that you *will* go. I love you too much to see you shrivel and fade. You are so vital, so young——'

'Well, I'm sorry, but you aren't getting that,' she said firmly. 'I love you, I'll always love you and in my book that means sticking it out through thick and thin. I'd rather be miserable with you than miserable without you.'

He stared at her for a long moment before a light sprang into his eyes at the same time as a wry smile touched the edge of his mouth. 'Is that a prediction for the future?'

'No.' She didn't return the smile. 'It is not. We are going to be happy, Francisco, very happy. I won't let it be any other way. And Carlos and the others, they will be glad for us, I know it.'

As he pulled her to him he covered her face in hard, feverish kisses which she answered with a passion that matched his, their bodies straining together in the limited confines of the car as they touched and fondled and caressed. She couldn't believe it. She couldn't take in that the nightmare of the last few hours was over and that he had come for her because he loved her.

'Why did you leave the castle?' He reached into the glove compartment and brought out the glittering little ornament carefully as he kept one arm wrapped round her. 'Was it because I had hurt you so badly?'

'No.' She looked at him as the sunlight turned her hair to silver. 'It was partly because I knew every time you looked at it it would remind you of me and I didn't want you to forget.'

'And?' he prompted gently.

'And because I didn't want to be put on a pedestal in a high tower,' she said slowly as she glanced at the little golden figure caught in the fine glass. 'I'm flesh and blood, Francisco, and I'm not waiting for a knight in shining armour; there's no need for me to do that.' The expression on her face spoke volumes.

'You are going to persist in seeing me as your knight,' he asked levelly, 'in spite of everything?' There was a pleading in the black eyes she knew he was unaware of, a need for reassurance.

'*Because* of everything,' she whispered softly. 'I love you, I respect you, you are everything I want——'

His mouth on hers cut off further conversation and it was several long, satisfying minutes later before either of them spoke again.

'I was a crazy man this morning,' he admitted quietly as he touched her hair with tender fingers. 'When I found you had gone I knew I could never let you go. It would have been the same at the airport or wherever we said goodbye. I could not have let it happen. And I realised I did not even know your address in England, only your surname and that you had a brother called Tom. It would have taken the army of private detectives I would have hired months to find you on that information.'

'You would have done that?' she asked in amazement.

'Of course.' The old arrogance was back now and she was actually thankful for it, she reflected wryly. She wanted him to be confident, contented, sure of himself...even arrogant if it meant the darkness was beginning to be banished.

'Will you marry me soon...or do you need time to be sure?' Just for a moment a spark of uncertainty coloured his face.

'Five seconds should do it,' she answered softly. 'Right, time's up, and yes, please, as soon as possible.'

'I will not be easy to live with although I will try.' He settled her against him again, her face against his chest and his arms holding her tight. 'But one thing I can promise you, my *infanta*— there will never be anyone else.'

'Likewise.' She raised her head, searching for his mouth, and after that further conversation seemed unnecessary.

# CHAPTER TEN

THEIR tenth wedding anniversary. Lorne glanced across at Francisco as he played in the water with Tom and the children, Tom's brood startlingly blond against the black hair and brown bodies of her own children. She had been thrilled and grateful for the instant bonding between the two men when they had first met at her wedding ten years ago, and their mutual appreciation of each other's personality had grown in the intervening years, Tom's family spending two or three holidays a year with them, always at Francisco's expense although Tom resisted every time.

'What are those big grey eyes thinking about?' Francisco asked softly as he joined her a few minutes later. 'Your husband, I hope?'

'What else?' She brushed his face with her hand as she spoke.

It had been several months before the nightmares had begun to ease, months of holding him close when he woke groaning and desperate in the night, his big body drenched with sweat and unspeakable horrors in his eyes. But ease they had as she had poured love and light and laughter into his life, banishing the darkness with a determination that she wouldn't have dreamt she was capable of.

185

Their first boy, born after two years of marriage, had been named Carlos, an unspoken decision they had both taken without discussion. The next one, a year later, Thomas Rodrigo after both their fathers. Little Francisco had been next and, just when she had given up all hope of ever producing the daughter she wanted so badly, last year little Amy Catalina had made their family complete, arriving to order on Lorne's own birthday.

She was so very fortunate. She glanced at Francisco as he lay back on the lounger at her side, his hand loosely linked in hers and his big, powerful body relaxed. He always needed to be able to see her, touch her, and for such an austere, reticent man she found it painfully touching.

She thought about the recent portrait he had completed of her and their daughter. It had been breathtakingly good and exquisitely sensitive, as had the ones with the boys in the previous years. She was glad he was able to paint again. She bent over and kissed the hard, firm mouth, protesting in giggling admonition as the muscled arms came out to hold her close to him. 'Francisco! There's Tom and Susie and the children...'

'No, there's only you.' The dark eyes held her fast and she drowned in their warmth as his hard body stirred beneath her.

The bad dreams had stopped after the birth of little Carlos but even now, at times, he would search for her in the warm darkness of their enormous bed, taking her with an urgency that spoke of inner torment, and she would reassure

him in the only way she knew how, giving of
herself so completely that he would relax in the
intensity of her love, of knowing that he was the
only man she would ever want, her knight in
black velvet.

# HEARTS OF FIRE

What will happen to Gemma now that Nathan seems determined
to end their marriage?

And can Celeste spend the rest of her life taking revenge on Byron
and building up her empire? Can she continue to deny all those
long-buried feelings?

**All will be revealed in…**

## SCANDALS & SECRETS
### by Miranda Lee

**Book 5 in the compelling HEARTS OF FIRE saga.**

Available from July 1994                    Priced: £2.50

## MILLS & BOON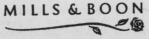

# THREE TIMES
# A LOVE STORY

A special collection of three individual love stories from one of the world's best-loved romance authors. This beautiful volume offers a unique chance for new fans to sample some of Janet Dailey's earlier works and for long-time fans to collect an edition to treasure.

# WORLDWIDE

AVAILABLE NOW                    PRICED £4.99

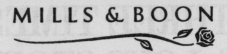

# MILLS & BOON

## HEARTS OF FIRE by Miranda Lee

Welcome to our compelling family saga set in the glamorous world of opal dealing in Australia. Laden with dark secrets, forbidden desires and scandalous discoveries, **Hearts of Fire** unfolds over a series of 6 books, but each book also features a passionate romance with a happy ending and can be read independently.

### Book 1: SEDUCTION & SACRIFICE
Published: April 1994        *FREE* with Book 2

*WATCH OUT for special promotions!*

Lenore had loved Zachary Marsden secretly for years. Loyal, handsome and protective, Zachary was the perfect husband. Only Zachary would never leave his wife…would he?

### Book 2: DESIRE & DECEPTION
Published: April 1994        Price £2.50

Jade had a name for Kyle Armstrong: *Mr Cool*. He was the new marketing manager at Whitmore Opals—the job *she* coveted. However, the more she tried to hate this usurper, the more she found him attractive…

### Book 3: PASSION & THE PAST
Published: May 1994        Price £2.50

Melanie was intensely attracted to Royce Grantham—which shocked her! She'd been so sure after the tragic end of her marriage that she would never feel for any man again. How strong was her resolve not to repeat past mistakes?

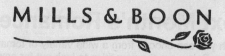

# MILLS & BOON

## HEARTS OF FIRE by Miranda Lee

### Book 4: FANTASIES & THE FUTURE
Published: June 1994          Price £2.50

The man who came to mow the lawns was more stunning than any of Ava's fantasies, though she realised that Vincent Morelli thought she was just another rich, lonely housewife looking for excitement! But, Ava knew that her narrow, boring existence was gone forever...

### Book 5: SCANDALS & SECRETS
Published: July 1994          Price £2.50

Celeste Campbell had lived on her hatred of Byron Whitmore for twenty years. Revenge was sweet...until news reached her that Byron was considering remarriage. Suddenly she found she could no longer deny all those long-buried feelings for him...

### Book 6: MARRIAGE & MIRACLES
Published: August 1994          Price £2.50

Gemma's relationship with Nathan was in tatters, but her love for him remained intact—she was going to win him back! Gemma knew that Nathan's terrible past had turned his heart to stone, and she was asking for a miracle. But it was possible that one could happen, wasn't it?

## Don't miss all six books!

*Available from WH Smith, John Menzies, Volume One, Forbuoys, Martins, Woolworths, Tesco, Asda, Safeway and other paperback stockists.*
*Also available from Mills & Boon Reader Service, FREEPOST, PO Box 236, Croydon, Surrey CR9 9EL (UK Postage & Packing free).*

# Next Month's Romances

Each month you can choose from a wide variety of romance with Mills & Boon. Below are the new titles to look out for next month, why not ask either Mills & Boon Reader Service or your Newsagent to reserve you a copy of the titles you want to buy – just tick the titles you would like and either post to Reader Service or take it to any Newsagent and ask them to order your books.

| *Please save me the following titles:* | Please tick | ✓ |
|---|---|---|
| THE SULTAN'S FAVOURITE | Helen Brooks | |
| INFAMOUS BARGAIN | Daphne Clair | |
| A TRUSTING HEART | Helena Dawson | |
| MISSISSIPPI MOONLIGHT | Angela Devine | |
| TIGER EYES | Robyn Donald | |
| COVER STORY | Jane Donnelly | |
| LEAP OF FAITH | Rachel Elliot | |
| EVIDENCE OF SIN | Catherine George | |
| THE DAMARIS WOMAN | Grace Green | |
| LORD OF THE MANOR | Stephanie Howard | |
| INHERITANCE | Shirley Kemp | |
| PASSION'S PREY | Rebecca King | |
| DYING FOR YOU | Charlotte Lamb | |
| NORAH | Debbie Macomber | |
| PASSION BECOMES YOU | Michelle Reid | |
| SHADOW PLAY | Sally Wentworth | |

If you would like to order these books in addition to your regular subscription from Mills & Boon Reader Service please send £1.90 per title to: Mills & Boon Reader Service, Freepost, P.O. Box 236, Croydon, Surrey, CR9 9EL, quote your Subscriber No:................................... (if applicable) and complete the name and address details below. Alternatively, these books are available from many local Newsagents including W H Smith, J Menzies, Martins and other paperback stockists from 12 August 1994.

Name:..............................................................................

Address:..........................................................................

...............................................Post Code:........................

**To Retailer: If you would like to stock M&B books please contact your regular book/magazine wholesaler for details.**

You may be mailed with offers from other reputable companies as a result of this application. If you would rather not take advantage of these opportunities please tick box. ☐